BELFIELD

BELFIELD

a novel

Joan Aleshire

GREEN WRITERS PRESS
Brattleboro, Vermont

10 9 8 7 6 5 4 3 2 1

Green Writers Press is a Vermont-based publisher whose mission is to spread a message of hope and renewal through the words and images we publish. Throughout we will adhere to our commitment to preserving and protecting the natural resources of the earth. To that end, a percentage of our proceeds will be donated to environmental and social-activist groups. Green Writers Press gratefully acknowledges support from individual donors, friends, and readers to help support the environment and our publishing initiative. Green Place Books curates books that tell literary and compelling stories with a focus on writing about place—these books are more personal stories/memoir and biographies.

Giving Voice to Writers & Artists Who Will Make the World a Better Place
Green Writers Press | Brattleboro, Vermont
www.greenwriterspress.com

ISBN: 979-8-9883820-7-2

The cover art is an adaptation by Vermont artist Grace Brigham of a sketch by Charles Willson Peale titled, "Belfield: The Mansion House," and contained in a letter reprinted in Charles Coleman Sellers' biography, *Charles Willson Peale*: New York: Charles Scribner's Sons, 1969

For my family.

BELFIELD

Belfield is an historical novel
based on the life of Charles Willson Peale.

Chapter 1

DUST OF EARLY SPRING IN THE ROAD, and the creak of a
wagon rounding the turn: they are here. The dogs rush
out, raising their usual alarm, and stop short at Charles
Willson's command for quiet, as he comes to greet these arrivals.

He's said they're payment for a portrait, that he'll accept anything, although Eliza argues it should be cash only. This time, his
neighbor's crop failed just after his sitting was finished, the paint
barely dry. *I'm forced to sell some land and other property. Maybe
you'll take this fine family*—a man and wife and their ten-year-old
son—*helpful around the house and yard?*

Charles Willson had hesitated; he doesn't like to order anyone around, except his children and all the strays attached to
his household, and has publicly opposed owning other human
beings. As a boy bound to a saddle-maker, he chafed against his
term of service, saw the slave markets on the docks in Baltimore's
harbor, and hurried past. He knows the cruelties inflicted on the
powerless; this man, woman and child have even less purchase on
life than he did as a criminal's son trying to make his way in the
New World. He thinks, *Surely, I can give them a better home.*

So, *Yes,* he said, striding now out to meet the wagon: a man in
his late fifties, with a substantial girth and strong, slender legs, a

keen eye. He grasps the man's arm to help him out of the wagon; the man winces, and when his feet hit the ground, he stumbles. He is tall and broad-shouldered, and holds his head as straight as he can, although it's clear he's suffered some injury to his neck. The purple scar of a brand or lash-mark can be seen where his shirt collar dips. Charles Willson puts out his right hand, but the man declines to shake it, and looks to the sky, as if to ask what strange place he's come to. Charles Willson doesn't press him to respond but reaches for the woman's hand as if she's a well-born white neighbor, not sepia-skinned, dust-covered, enslaved. She rises and steps from the wagon-seat unaided, her shoulders hunched forward as if to hide her breasts and belly.

Like Lydia: Charles Willson is lost a moment, remembering that other woman once in his household. The neighbor, still holding the horse's reins—he doesn't intend to linger—looks at Charles Willson with the sting of condescension the well-born seem born with: "They're here to work, not be your guests. It never pays to be too kind. . . ."

But Charles Willson turns away with a flap of his hand, as the boy in the back of the wagon jumps up with the three small bundles of his family's belongings and slides to the ground. For a moment, before Charles Willson cuffs his shoulder—"Welcome, boy!"—and leads him inside, the boy catches the eye of a girl in the window sewing a button on a large white shirt.

She sees a boy about her own age, the color of the sunlit wooden windowsill, thin and with a head shaved so close the shaving must have been painful. He doesn't meet her look after this instant of forgetfulness; he looks at his bare, ashy feet, grasps the bundles tighter, and follows his parents and this new white man down the hallway to the kitchen.

The girl herself hasn't been here long. Although she has white skin, she hardly belongs in this house full of children named for famous artists, learning to be artists themselves under their father's demanding eye. Like the dogs and horses and the five-legged, six-footed cow he rescued from beatings and starvation, Charles Willson found her not doing what was wanted, or not doing what was wanted well enough: holding out her basket of seeded coins to passers-by, showing her misshapen hand. She was crying when Charles Willson turned down her street; a woman had just pulled her skirts away with a look of disgust, as if whatever afflicted the child would touch her with contagion.

"Where do you live?" he'd asked, putting coins meant for dinner into her basket. She'd sobbed too hard to answer, able only to point in the direction of the corner shop. The wine merchant, who'd looked up with a practiced eye at Charles Willson's approach, drew back, explaining himself: "I said I'd take her; no one else would. . .I said I'd find something she can do, but she can't even do that. . ."

"Where's her family?"

The wine-seller waved his hand in the direction of far-away: "Dead or don't want her. I worked for her father; took her to pay off a debt."

"If I take her, will anyone come looking?"

The other man leered: "She's pretty young, but if you put some flesh on her. . ."

Charles Willson coughed into his hand to hide his disgust. If truth be told, he was insulted: a man of his imposing height and keen eye thinks he can have any woman he wants. Without looking at the wine-seller, "Get your things," he said to the girl.

Used to following orders, she flew up the stairs without hesitation, banging the basket with its few coins, put into it her extra set of under-linens, her other dress, and the curry comb she uses for her hair. Later she'll wonder at her immediate assent that's more than mere obedience; there was a strange hope in it. Charles Willson has that effect on almost everyone; it's how he went from being bound to a saddler to teaching himself to paint, to persuading generals and presidents he can paint them as well as West and better than Stuart.

In the trap behind a single, lively horse, sitting beside this man who smells of tobacco and a bit of lavender, she wonders where he'll take her but has no fear that it will be worse than where she's been. She can't of course remember the darkened birthing room and the woman whose body she's come from screaming: "Maisie, get her away from me!" and brown arms carrying her, swaddling her—the cord's stump still bleeding—to a wagon jolting, not far, and murmuring voices, outstretched hands holding her tight, before the warm brown arms take her again and hold her to a bared breast.

The man next to her in the trap seems to have taken her in without looking at her directly; he shifts slightly so as not to crowd her partial hand's hold on the basket. He drops the reins to the horse's back and jiggles them, clucking; she sees there's no whip. The horse picks her way over the slippery cobbles, and moves freely as they head west on the dirt highway to greening fields edged with trees, grazing cows and horses, barns and out-buildings, houses and gardens.

He says by way of introduction: "I have two daughters about your age. We'll find what you like to do and help you do it well."

She doesn't know how to answer, but he doesn't seem to expect her to, guiding the horse down an elm-lined lane, which opens onto a house that seems to float on the grass. She sees a flash of white in a dormer window, as if someone has been watching who doesn't want to be seen; then two spaniels or retrievers come rushing from somewhere, barking with joy, not alarm.

The man turns to her: "I haven't asked your name."

"Mag." She's so unused to speaking that the word comes as a whisper.

"Short for?"

"Mar'gret," the syllables crowd together in her dry mouth.

"What do you like to be called?" So surprised to be asked that she can't answer, her silence is lost in the small crowd of boys who come out of different doors to take the horse's bridle and greet their father. Two young girls come running too, and stop at the sight of her.

"Father, what did you bring?" The taller girls asks.

"A friend to live with us," he answers. "Have you finished your lessons? Can you show her to one of the upstairs rooms?"

Her legs are stiff; she's afraid she won't be able to stand or will drop her basket and spill her clothes in front of everyone.

"Here," the smaller girl says, taking the basket. "You can come with me. Father, you've never said her name." When Mag's misshapen hand uncurls from the basket-handle, the other girl pauses to notice its strangeness, but, like her father, moves on briskly toward the house. "Come on."

"I'm Mag," she allows to the other, who half-turns, smiles. "I'm Sophonisba, or Isba, if *Sophonisba* seems too long."

The taller girl, clearly feeling that her younger sister is taking over the new arrival, says, "And I'm Angelica. We don't shorten it."

The boys—Raphaelle, Rembrandt and Titian—stare at her with barely concealed curiosity, until their father prompts: "Are you statues or young gentlemen?" At which they bow and say their unusual names.

The room that will be hers, until she leaves this house for her own, has the deep eaves of a sharply cut dormer; her bed, with its mended quilt, seems protected by its wings. She puts her belongings in the chest under the window, and the stones Maisie told her were lucky—gray with a white band—on the sill. The girls will say she has the worst room—hot in summer, dark in winter—but she feels safe there, and wouldn't change if she could.

"Come down to dinner!" Isba is in the doorway. "But you'll need to wash up first," leading Mag to a bright room lined with shelves—a library of preserves and bottled drink—with a hand-pump and metal sink by the door. Isba pulls the handle, and Mag understands that she's to cup her good hand under the shocking cold flow, and clean her dusty face. Isba laughs at their success and brushes Mag's hair back from her face and smooths it.

Voices come from another room: a woman's, with a quarrelsome edge: "But you can't have brought her here!" and a man's lower answer: "She's here."

"But what can she do? There's too much work already, without having to stop to help a cripple."

"She can be taught."

"You think even dumb animals can learn something," the woman says in exasperation, and the man doesn't answer, thinking not for the first time that he didn't choose this second wife as well as he might have: Elizabeth DePeyster, from an old Dutch family, and too proud of it.

He stands at the pantry door, pleased to see Isba wiping Mag's face. "Come, girls, to dinner."

Mag has never seen such a profusion of food, even in her grandmother's house when she was very young: bowls of steaming new peas, bowls of berries, jugs of cream, platters of asparagus stacked like small logs. A white woman with hair as white as her cap carries in the roast: "Ready to carve it up, Charles Willson?"

A bell is struck somewhere, and the room fills: the boys she's met; Angelica; a tall blonde woman with a discontented expression; an old woman in a wheeled chair pushed by one of the boys; a man who looks like Charles Willson, only thinner, shorter: the Peale family as he'll paint it at that moment, including one of the retrievers waiting patiently for scraps.

She squeezes into a chair between Isba and one of her brothers, who moves his arm, not to touch hers. No one speaks or moves until Charles Willson says, "Bless this food to our use, and us to thy service," swiftly: a nod to tradition more than an invocation, before he begins to slice the roast with a flourish of his knife, giving to each the portion he thinks they need. "Eliza, my dear:" he hands out her plate, in a tone the endearment doesn't soften. "Mother," Margaret Peale, is next; her meat, Mag sees, he's carefully cut into small pieces, and is surprised that her own plate is passed around next: "Our new arrival, Mag."

Charles Willson has quietly cut her beef, too, into fine rectangles, and looks at her to see her nod in recognition, not quite gratitude. She'd learned to cut her meat quite well at her grandmother's house, pinning the pieces with her fingerless right hand, wielding the knife in her left. No one then tried to correct her, or thought she couldn't cut her food for herself—certainly not her grandmother, who'd said when she was a year old: "This is the brightest child I've ever seen," slighting her own children and grandchildren.

Here, if anyone might stare or even mimic or mock her way of cutting things, Charles Willson hasn't given them the chance. And the boys are too busy to notice her, making sure they get their share as the plates get passed down the table: "Raphaelle;" "Rembrandt;" "Rubens;" Titian." The peas and potatoes come next in large bowls. Isba, who seems to grasp instantly what Mag needs (and will take pride in this), holds the bowls for her as she scoops vegetables to her plate.

When the horseradish comes, grated into a small glass dish, she takes hold of it, sets it down in the open space by her plate, and gives herself a heaping helping before passing it on. Her grandmother's kitchen never sent out anything so spicy; she takes too much, struggles to keep from choking, and can't stop the tears.

Angelica, across the table, begins to laugh, but stops abruptly— almost as if someone has kicked her—before her father can say her name with the note of censure she hates. Under the table,

Isba hands Mag a handkerchief from her pocket; the lavender scent makes her sneeze, as the kindness makes her cry harder.

She pushes back her chair. She hasn't let herself miss her grandmother's house since the day the shutters were kept closed, her grandmother's coffin was carried out, the household's servants stood hushed, some in tears. Her grandmother had always called them *servants*, never *slaves*, and never showed how sick she was, the months she grew thinner and had to try hard to smile. She never was less than kind or showed strain, but how little she owned was clear when the tall men came in black suits—her sons and lawyers—and said the property would be sold, which meant the humans, too. Mag's uncles argued over her, without caring that she could hear. One agreed to take her, but was drunk when he did and hadn't even gotten her home before he'd given her to the wine-seller to pay his debt.

In this new place, on the narrow bed under the eaves, she can't imagine that anything good will come of her, *for* her. She hadn't closed the door behind her; Isba knocks on the frame: "Aren't you hungry?" She carries Mag's full plate; Angelica is behind her, with a fork and glass.

"Father wants you to come down, at least for dessert. There's berries and cake for Rubens' birthday. He's usually in the garden, but he washed up for his dinner."

That no one says *No* to Charles Willson, Mag knows without having to be told.

She smooths her mussed hair, wipes her face dry with her heel of a hand, and follows the Peale sisters downstairs, where Peggy is carrying in the cake.

"We wish you a happy birthday, a joyous and glorious bir-r-r-th-day, dear Rubens! May you have a long life!" Everyone but Mag sings; it's a song different from the one her grandmother's household sang to her. So much attention embarrasses Rubens;

he'd rather be planting his lettuces or pulling radishes from the dirt, but he can't hide a smile of pleasure or refuse to blow the fifteen candles out.

"Wish! Wish! What do you wish?" the girls and Titian taunt.

"Won't tell," Rubens answers, cutting them smaller slices of the cake.

After dinner, Angelica opens the harpsichord; Isba and Raphaelle will sing, but Mag is too tired to listen. She can hardly climb the narrow stairs to her bed, and falls asleep in her clothes. When she wakes to a shaft of moonlight, she's glad to find a basin of water on a stand, and a chamber pot under it. Through the many-paned window she sees the moon silvering the garden rows and the apple trees below. "Belfield," Charles Willson called it, as he turned the trap into the drive. "Our ark," he added to himself.

Chapter 2

I T'S BARELY LIGHT WHEN THE HOUSE COMES ALIVE; there are footsteps in the hall, the sound of water being pumped, smells of bread and coffee rising from the kitchen.

Mag washes her face, wishes for a mirror, looks over the dress she's brought, but finds it too crumpled to be more presentable than the soiled one she has on. There's nothing for it but to go downstairs, wondering where the chamber pot's contents should go.

The room with the long dining table is empty, but voices come from the pantry and kitchen. Isba and Angelica come forward and take her by both (both!) hands.

The woman who'd carried in the roast the night before is stirring something on the stove, moving the pot off the hottest part of the fire and opening the draft.

"This is Mag," Isba says; the woman reaches out with her right hand, sees how misshapen Mag's is, and shakes it anyway. "I'm Peggy." She sets a bowl of oatmeal on the work table. "There's butter and cream for it, and honey. Coffee for you? Charles Willson has had his; Eliza is dressing her hair. I don't know where the boys are this morning."

Mag manages to pull the honey from its jar, not caring how

sticky her hand is getting or whether someone will try to correct her or take over the task. Like Charles Willson, Peggy and the girls notice without staring or taking exception. Grateful, she eats the rich mess slowly and holds the bowl of coffee-with-milk with both hands, her face bathed by its steam.

"Girls," Peggy says over her shoulder, "I've started the fires under the wash-pots. When you finish eating, we'll strip the beds and put the linens in to soak. Mag, you'll work with Isba. Angelica, what you can't do on your own, I'll help with."

There are so many beds in this house, and so many linens to be washed, that they divide and rotate which rooms they'll do; the wash-pots are always steaming.

Today: Grandmother's room, which is also Peggy's; Eliza's, with the big canopied bed; Charles Willson's dressing room with the cot. Tomorrow: Rembrandt and Raphaelle's; Rubens and Titian's. Wednesday: Angelica and Isba's; and Mag's. If anyone else comes to stay in the attic rooms, the washing will take an extra day. The birthing room is vacant now, but will fill soon, when Eliza's baby comes. Rosalba's empty cradle is still there, with her rose-colored quilt.

Stirring sheets heavy with boiling wash-water in large cast-iron pots: calling on one's God won't help if one tips over. Isba does most of the stirring at first, but Mag finds her stronger arm strong enough for the work if her weaker one supports it. She's proud when Peggy nods, coming to help all three girls pull the hot sheets out and twist them as dry as possible. Only her large hands can do this, though Angelica helps with the ends. All four of them carry each twisted sheet to the new mangle Charles Willson has brought home, and feeds them in. Damp, most of the water squeezed out, the girls spread them on the hedges that rim the garden.

Mag is delegated to shoo birds away and watch for rain, while Angelica and Isba take clean sheets from the linen closet to make the stripped beds again. Mag volunteers to help, seeing no clouds in the sky and thinking birds will be more interested in the currant bushes nearby. She's aware she's been given the easiest job.

She and Isba are unfolding a sheet, lavender scent rising around them, in Eliza's room, when Eliza comes to the door. Her hair is combed in a high pouf above her pale face; she sways slightly and puts a hand to the door frame. "How soon will you be done?"

Isba slaps the sheet hard instead of smoothing it. "Soon," she answers.

"Don't you need someone else to help you?" Eliza clearly means *other than Mag*, who feels the stare on her right hand and protectively puts it behind her. "Where's Angelica?"

"Helping Peggy do Grandmother's room," Isba says without looking at her stepmother, motioning to Mag to hold the sheet's edge. Together they raise it high, like a billowing sail, and bring it down, Mag holding onto one end with her complete hand, grasping the other between her partial hand and her waist.

"Mind you don't drop it," Eliza nods toward Mag. Eliza's clear belief that she *will* drop it, dirty it, makes Mag lose her own belief that whatever comes, she can figure out a way to do it. She trembles, half in fear, half in anger, which Isba feels along the length of sheet.

"Don't you need to sit down?" she asks Eliza with an unmistakable hint of condescension. Young as she is, Isba knows how uncertain her stepmother is in her mother's place, with a family that's existed for years before she came into it and a husband supremely confident of his own beliefs and gifts. And still, she suspects, in love with the wife who died: Rachel, whose portrait hangs in the dining room over every meal, whose spirit lives with the family still, whose daughters' faces, voices, and every gesture recall her.

Eliza sits heavily on a chair that creaks under her. Mag feels a pang of sympathy, which won't dispel her sense of how the woman regards her: as an offense to the order she wants to have around her.

As Isba slams the blanket onto the wide bed, Mag sees tears in her eyes about to spill. She tugs the blanket toward her side twice, as a signal: *I know. I see.* Isba tugs back, and the unending work is almost done for the morning.

Lunch at Belfield can be more like dinner, with guests and a full meal, or can be a quick pause from work, like this day, with a tureen of vegetable soup, a chunk of cheddar and hard crackers that Raphaelle will paint so close to life that, when it's set on an exhibition table, someone will reach for a knife.

The girls bring bowls and plates from the cabinet. Mag takes only a few pieces at a time, but steps quickly as she goes back and forth, to keep up with the rest. Peggy watches her without seeming to, then calls out: "Rubens, mind your boots!" as the boy stumbles in with mud to his ankles, dazed from his morning in the garden.

Charles Willson rushes in, flings down his box of paints and his jacket, cross from a difficult sitting. He's been in the city, painting Eliza's parents, who keep stopping him to see how he's doing, suggesting changes to make their thick features more refined. He has to struggle not to offend them but can't betray his own observant eyes. He'll slip some sign of his distaste into the background. A goose counting coins would be too obvious, but that's the temptation.

Rembrandt and Raphaelle gulp their soup and take crackers and chunks of cheese to the gaming table, where they continue, quarreling, their game of chess. Titian leans over Rembrandt's chair. Rubens stays at the table, eating slowly, still in a green haze and so near-sighted he misses Mag's attempt to pass him the butter dish, which she can't hold long enough and, to her horror, lets fall.

The porcelain lands softly on oak; Charles Willson looks up from his soup and smiles at her, making clear that there are more important things in this house than unbroken china. Mag, who had started to push back her chair, stays in her place with an exhaled breath that the sisters share.

Rubens hasn't noticed the small domestic drama, and Angelica nudges his arm: "Mag was passing you the butter."

"I don't want any," he answers, not looking up, and the girls, even Mag, begin to laugh: Angelica and Isba because Rubens is being so typically Rubens; Mag in the sudden ease of feeling she belongs there.

Charles Willson's younger brother, James, comes as the girls are clearing the dishes—Mag carrying only what she can and moving fast. James goes to the kitchen for his coffee before beginning the lessons. The boys are reading Caesar in the original; the girls are starting their Latin declensions and ask Mag what she wants to learn. She knows how to read, and can write a little with her left hand since she lived at her grandmother's house. She'll practice penmanship, James decides, and then try one of the early grade readers.

After lunch, he'll lead them all in singing; then each one who's chosen an instrument will play in turn. When they range around the harpsichord, with James at the keyboard beginning a Mozart air, Mag tries to sing with them but fails to stay in tune. She stands silent and miserable, not knowing the German words, or she would mouth them, and not hearing the notes. James, after the first song, calls an intermission and edges her aside: "I'll work with you another day." He's noticed that playing an instrument would take more fingers than she has; he suggests she find a book she likes in the library, and he'll help her read it, if she wants.

"The library?" She hasn't yet seen the room with books covering the walls.

She tiptoes where James points, finding Charles Willson

stretched out on a sofa that barely holds his length and width, with a handkerchief gently rising and falling over his face. As quietly and carefully as she can, she pulls a heavy leather folder from a low shelf and kneels to open it: *Leonardo da Vinci: Drawings*: thick pages of inked images she turns as gently as she can.

She can't help going too fast, afraid someone will tell her to stop or call her back to lessons. She's as lost in lines and circles, a hand, the shape of a man, as Rubens is in his garden, and doesn't hear Charles Willson stir or the notebook open on his waistcoat slip to the floor.

"Do you like those?" Mag is so startled she drops the box, scattering the pages across the rug. Charles Willson kneels beside her, gathering them up: "I haven't looked at these since I did them; it's good to see them again."

"*You* did them?" She's too shaken to be aware she's being rude, but Charles Willson doesn't take offense:

"Learned from copying the originals; Leonardo was a good teacher," he says as if he'd known the artist, as if he's still alive, and, for Charles Willson, this is true.

"It must be hard to do. . . . " She can't imagine how anyone could make such faces and hands rise out of flat paper.

"Not if you love doing it: if you let what you see flow through your hand onto the page." He lines up the pages they've gathered and returns them to the leather box. "I think that's all of them: no harm done. In time, you'll find what you love to do and do it. I can help."

Drawing and painting lessons begin as soon as Charles Willson has had another coffee from the silver pot with the olive-wood handle. The coffee is cold by this time of day, but it gives him the clarity he needs. The schoolroom fills with afternoon light, dust motes floating, golden, in it. Angelica is the model today; the others take their places at their easels. Titian is missing when they begin, but his brothers, sister, and Mag bend to the work, studying the way Angelica's arm stretches along the arm of a chair, and the angle of her neck. They all keep an eye on their father, who's drawing along with them. From time to time, he walks among them, adjusting a hand's position here, a line there, but gently; he wants to encourage their eyes to see more clearly, their hands to move more surely.

He doesn't criticize and, this day, doesn't question Titian's whereabouts; he's unsurprised, even welcoming, when the boy comes, cradling a dead baby mouse in his hands. "Can I draw this?" "Is it dead?" Angelica asks. Nodding, Titian has already put the small body on the table and taken up his charcoal.

The drawing lesson is short; no one can complain of being bored. Peggy has cocoa keeping warm on the coals and cookies cooling on racks. "We'll need the lettuces picked for dinner, and the peas. Any of you girls want to help make rolls?"

Peggy throws a lump on the bread board; it springs back like a living thing as she kneads. Isba and Mag lean on the counter beside her. "Can we pinch it?" Peggy shows them how much to pinch and how to pat each ball into the metal forms.

Angelica beats the eggs for custard, lets them stay on the hot fire only long enough to thicken. Peggy's plucked the chickens, thrown the entrails into the dogs' bowl, wields the cleaver to wing-tips and neck, which go into the pot always simmering on the hearth.

The fire must be hot at first, then banked under the oven as the rolls bake. Peggy shows Mag when to open the door to bring the heat down. The smell of bread fills the kitchen almost at once; it's easy to get so lost in it, the batch can be lost, Peggy explains, seeing by Mag's expression that she's already entranced. When Charles Willson asks her what she loves, one day at a drawing lesson, she'll say, "Being in the kitchen." One of the boys snickers, but their father answers: "Cookery too is one of the arts," and she's encouraged to spend as much time there as she wants, learning how to do what Peggy does: not exactly *how* she does it, or even exactly well, but well enough. Peggy tolerates her blunders, glad of the company and the bit of help.

Chapter 3

WHEN LUCY and Scarborough come to Belfield with their son, the kitchen is the first place they're led to, through a dark hallway and into the large room, where they stand, holding the bundles of their belongings, dazed by the light that streams through the tall windows and unsure what is expected of them. Peggy, too, is unsure: how to treat them, what their place will be. This is a moment when everything is still: when the future of their time in this house will be determined.

Peggy, whose mother and Margaret Peale were sisters, and who married worse than her mother, remembers the Baltimore market where naked brown men and women, even children, were bought and sold. On her way to run some errand—often begging credit from the shops—she would hurry down another street to avoid the sight of those sales; she couldn't block out the hawkers' voices and crude laughter, no matter which street she took. She's heard Charles Willson criticize Washington, Jefferson, and even Franklin for owning people, and wonders where these people have come from, and why they're here. She holds out her hand: "I'm Peggy."

The man, Scarborough, gives her a quizzical look, as if to say: *What world you been living in?* and then catches himself:

"Scarborough, ma'am." Peggy is tall, but he is taller, thin and muscular; he takes her white hand, and she notices the wide purple scar running around the base of his thumb. Mag, who has just come in, sees a man with high cheekbones, searching eyes, and deep brown skin. "This is my wife, Lucy," he says, just as a white neighbor would—he's spent years noticing—"and this is our son, Moses."

Lucy looks as if she's about to faint, her smooth tan face crumpling as she reaches for a chair-back. "Mag, get her a glass of water," Peggy says, and sets bread and cheese on the kitchen table. "Please sit." Lucy looks as if an overseer will come to drag her away to whatever punishment house they have here, but Scar pulls out the bench and motions to her: "It's all right."

Moses comes closer, and Peggy says: "You can put your bundle down. It's not quite lunchtime, but you look as if you could use some soup." She wants to ask: "Do you know kitchens?" but not just yet, not until she knows what Charles Willson is planning.

Mag brings bowls from the cabinet and hands one to Peggy, who ladles the soup—mostly carrots and onions today—into the bowl Mag grasps in her good left hand, supporting the hot china with her right, trying to keep the boiling liquid from touching her skin. From across the room, the boy Moses moves next to her, lifting the bowl from her hands into his so carefully, she hardly knows how he's done it without spilling a drop, not asking anything or giving her directions: simply by paying attention. They've acted in such concert, it's as if they're one person.

The late morning sun falling on the kitchen table has turned Lucy's red-brown hair to spun gold, the brand on Scarborough's bent neck a more violent red, and their boy's round face brighter in the soup's steam. In all their long lives, Mag will see him as she does this first time: his quick glance up at her, mischief tugging the corners of his mouth before he turns to the food, his long slender fingers that took the soup bowl from her so deftly breaking the chunk of bread. His dusty feet under the kitchen bench seem so in need of protection she wants to hold them.

She's so lost in watching them she's as startled as Scarborough and Lucy are—Scarborough jumping to his feet and letting his spoon drop to his plate—when Charles Willson comes into the room with his usual gust of confidence and authority.

"You're getting settled, I see? Peggy, can you show them the corner attic room, the one with the big bed?" Scarborough flinches, as if some crude remark or leer will follow, but Charles Willson takes no notice, intent on giving directions: "And the boy can have one of the smaller rooms. Mag, have you been comfortable enough up there?"

She doesn't say how hot it gets in the late afternoons, even now in early spring, or how hard it is for her to sleep, worrying, against all evidence, what hardship will strike her here.

"Enough," she says, with nothing to soften it—and he moves on to the next item on his list of concerns, barely seeming to hear her. Later, when he asks if she'd like to move to a second-floor room with Isba, she realizes that he takes in more than he seems to. This day his benevolence is on full display: "Scarborough and Lucy, when you get settled, and the boy, we'll talk about what you'd like to do."

Lucy looks up at him, just a beat long enough to register her skepticism; Charles Willson notices this, and also that she's a beautiful woman, if a bit unwell, maybe pregnant, certainly exhausted. She turns her shoulders in to protect her body; *Lydia,* he thinks again. Scarborough frowns, then nods: "Yes, sir," but his movements are dismissive; he turns back to his soup.

Peggy says: "I could use more help in the kitchen; there are a lot of people to feed."

And Charles Willson asks Scarborough and Lucy: "Do you know kitchens?"

Mag is pinching a bit of dough out of the bowl for the next

day's starter when she hears voices on the porch, low but distinct, even through the violin and harpsichord beginning a lesson in the living room: Eliza's querulous: "We can't have them eating with us or sleeping in the same house," and Charles Willson's: "Where would you have them go, Miss?" Then a chair scrapes, and Charles Willson is in the kitchen: "Mag, make sure there are three more places at the table."

In the end, there are four empty chairs at the evening meal: Eliza's—she begs an upset stomach; and Scarborough's, Lucy's, and Moses's. They couldn't have heard Eliza's indignant question but have stayed in their rooms, exhausted by the journey, dislocated in this strange new place.

The Peale boys bicker as usual, the girls chatter as they serve and clear; Peggy urges Margaret to try a little turnip mash. Only Mag notices how unusually quiet Charles Willson is until his brother James comes, late as usual, and serves himself from the sideboard. Charles Willson teases James that he's making up for all the hungry years of their childhood, and James laughs, although he has a harder time dismissing that early pain than his brother does.

They talk of what they know of Pennsylvania's manumission laws, but they don't know much, having thought only of abolition. James has heard something about freedom being contingent on the ability to make a living; and rumors of roving bounty hunters with no boundaries.

"I can't see keeping them," Charles Willson says. "But now I have them, I'll have to figure out how." He fills his glass with claret—the time he'll drink only spring water is still in the future—and goes out as soon as the meal is over. From her upstairs window, Eliza will see his horse's tail swinging as he gallops down the lane.

Chapter 4

THE HORSE SEEMS TO REMEMBER THE WAY, although his rider hasn't traveled that road for a while. Charles Willson pulls up at a glittering house in the center of the city; candlelight shines from every window although it's not quite dusk. A young Black man in livery comes to hold the horse's bridle: "Who are you here to see tonight, sir?"

"Is Mrs. Falconer in?"

"Your name, sir? I'll see if she's here."

Charles Willson fumbles in his pocket for his calling card. During the war, and often when Rachel was too busy being a mother, he was such a familiar presence here that everyone knew him on sight, and he knew everyone by name, even the girls he never patronized, spending his time only with the owner of the house. "Mrs. Falconer" she called herself, although many suspected she'd made up a long-ago marriage, and the grandeur of her first name: *Gloriana*, as if in ironic homage to the Virgin Queen. Grandeur suits her, and this evening, as soon as she's seen Charles Willson's card, she brushes the young doorkeeper aside and flings open the front door in a rush of violet scent, rustling silk and lavender powder.

"Charles Willson!" She embraces him hard enough to remind

him of her breasts, then holds him at arms' length, bracelets chiming. "It's been too long." She takes in the added weight that shows in his face, that makes him seem more a man of substance than the captain in Washington's army with the rakish cap and the wine jug slung from his shoulder. More settled than the young husband chafing at the restrictions of marriage. "What brings you?"

Now an upright citizen who criticizes soldiers for spending their pay on *prostytutes*, he nevertheless hasn't forgotten his ability to charm. "Wanting to see you," he answers.

Her rooms are as he remembers them in low light: the silk-covered sofa, the mahogany writing desk, the table with its crystal goblets and porcelain dishes, the doorway giving a glimpse of the four-poster bed piled with silk pillows and a puff of quilt.

He sits with her for what seems a long time, letting her refill his glass with wine; part of what he loves is the way she listens: as if there is no time, or only *this* time, and no other people except this man before this woman, telling her what he's told no one. How ill at ease he is to have a family of enslaved people in his household. How Eliza has encouraged him to buy more. How angry she is that he took in Mag, whom she calls *another useless feeder*.

If this dilemma makes Gloriana smile a bit cynically, if she's getting tired and wonders when she'll get to bed, even if they'll go together, she's trained herself too well to show opinions or strong emotions. She keeps her heart out of all her transactions but this one, with Charles Willson, who is more honest than he is rich, and more attentive than important. Sometimes on past nights she's told him her real name—*Morning Glory*—and of the island she never forgot and whose cadences inflect her speech. Once she talked of the careless men who'd bought and sold her; and the powerful one who bought this house for her for his own pleasure, and saw how, with care, she became the doyenne of one of his most lucrative businesses. Charles Willson makes her feel like telling; he listens.

Bed is for both of them somehow the least of it: which is not to say that it isn't pleasurable: once her copper hair springs from her formal wig, stays are unlaced, her high bosom falls into its natural shape, her skirts fall around her ankles; once he kicks off his boots, strips off his shirt, unbuttons his breeches, until they stand bare to each other: his sun-and-wind-reddened whiteness touching her smooth, golden brownness. In roughly two hundred years, women who look like her will be famous for their art and beauty. In 1785, men come to her only in secret and pay for her company; even they will often step back a moment, as Charles Willson does, to marvel at her. Except that Charles Willson has never had to pay; often he brought wine, perfume, blackberries from the farm. Tonight, he came in such a hurry, he hardly knew where he was going, and shows his empty hands.

She's learned new ways to please him, he's surprised to see, although her repertoire was large before. It's well into the new day, though not yet dawn, when he takes his leave. Before he goes, she searches for a card in her desk and slips it in her pocket. He raises his eyebrows in question, but she merely nods and gives him an affectionate if firm push of farewell.

The doorkeeper, who's been dozing in a chair by the door, hands him his hat; the groom, always on call, brings his horse. A few other men are leaving as he does; they nod without speaking or acknowledging that they may know one another in daylight.

Chapter 5

MAG THINKS SHE'S THE ONLY ONE who sees Charles Willson returning; she hasn't been able to sleep for the sobs that can't be muffled, coming from the corner room where Lucy and Scarborough stay. She doesn't know until he taps on her door that Moses, too, has been awake, his face streaked with tears. Without hesitating, she pulls him into her room and closes the door.

"It's Mama," he gasps. "She's bleeding."

Mag will run for Peggy—Margaret Peale, sleeping on her good ear, doesn't wake—and will collide with Charles Willson in the second-floor hall, rubbing his forehead as if to bring forth a solution. It comes: "I'm off to find Antigua and Yarrow. They'll help, and then I'll ride for the doctor." Ten miles back into the city, the way he's come; he'll have to take a fresh horse.

Antigua and Yarrow Mahmout live on the next farm over: free, working for themselves to make a garden famous in the neighborhood for its herbs and African vegetables. Charles Willson will paint Yarrow one day—his only portrait of an African American and one that shows the greatest warmth between painter and sitter—but this earliest morning, as he rides crossfields through the mist, startling the cows sleeping in the corner grove, he remembers how Yarrow got that name: from the herb that stopped the bleeding in the last battle of the War. Yarrow's mother used the remedy—some said she was a witch, even as they consulted her—for his boyhood cuts and scratches; and for women, including herself, after childbirth. Yarrow has said that his mother saved his life at Yorktown, and although white soldiers laughed at what they took to be his "simple-mindedness," they came to realize the truth of what he said. Charles Willson had never doubted him. He knocks now on the door of the cabin near the big house with a cautious urgency, hoping to wake only the people inside.

"Mr. Peale!" Yarrow steps aside and ushers him in, then, learning his errand, shows him to the small kitchen garden. Under Yarrow's lamp: a profusion of silver-grey, slightly fuzzy segmented leaves and spandrels of pale pink and yellow blossoms. "You strip the leaves off the stem and chew them for the quickest relief. Someone there can make a tea, steeping leaves and flowers together." At Charles Willson's skeptical look, Yarrow continues: "Worked for me."

Antigua is in the doorway in her nightdress. "Is it for a man or a woman?" and learning a woman, reaches for a bundle of dried leaves handing from a rafter: "Raspberry leaves for contractions, and to bring out the afterbirth."

"Can you use a chicken?" Charles Willson asks, and at Antigua's nod, says, "I'll send one of my boys over with one tomorrow."

He rides home toward the rising light; behind him, Antigua and Yarrow's lamp goes out; the big house stays dark and quiet. Farther west, unseen over the hills: the Randolph farm that sent him Scarborough and Lucy: the young owner sent north from Virginia, having disgraced his famous name with his drinking and gambling, bringing with him his pretensions, an anxious young wife, tobacco plants and enslaved workers.

At Belfield, only the third-floor windows show light; he takes the stairs as fast as he can, tired as he is, and finds Scarborough lit by the lamp behind him. "Yarrow?" he asks, taking the uprooted plants from Charles Willson, and, as the white man who by law owns him advises: "She'll need to chew the leaves," nods impatiently.

He already knows the remedy and, as the two men stand together—one in his urgency and his knowledge; the other in his ignorance and uncertainty—they achieve a curious equality. Both will understand later that an imbalance was slightly righted, an equilibrium achieved; they will regard each other a bit differently after this.

"Should I ride for the doctor?" Charles Willson asks, prepared in his exhaustion to do that. *Lydia* comes into his mind unbidden, Lydia, who never had the chance of a doctor.

Scarborough—the taller man, they're both aware—is the one giving directions at this moment in this house. "I expect this will work, but I'll let you know. Raspberry leaves in the bag?"

It's now so close to dawn that Charles Willson decides he may as well stay awake. He can't imagine how Eliza will react to his night-long absence, or what he can say to her that won't be a lie. He finds Peggy building a high fire on the hearth. "She was only five months gone; there was a baby as perfect as you'd find anywhere." She turns to the kettle. "And more white than brown." Charles Willson sits heavily on the hearth-side bench. "I'll get your coffee going, Charles Willson, but we have a lot of blood to clean up."

Mag comes with an armful of snowy cloths and the expression of someone stunned by what she's seen. "Hurry up with those, love," Peggy says.

"Will she be all right?" He's surprised by his own trembling. *At least this time he offered to call the doctor.*

"Most likely the yarrow will slow the bleeding, and you brought raspberry leaves? A tea of those will help her push any clots out."

Mag thinks of the red flood pouring from Lucy with a tiny doll-like unmoving figure floating on it. Perfectly shaped with a tiny cleft between its legs, it looked like the baby in Charles Willson's painting "Grief"—of Rachel and the few-months-old Rosalba that hangs on his painting-room wall, except that that baby wasn't covered in blood.

She wishes there were something she could do to stop Lucy from moaning, Moses from crying without making a sound, the bloody clumps coming from Lucy's body like chunks of meat. Peggy touches her shoulder: "I'll need help with the tea and the cleaning things."

When she goes back upstairs with the raspberry leaf tea, she finds Lucy asleep, Moses beside her, and Scar opening the shutters to morning. A blanket wraps the baby so its terrible still face can't be seen; there's no more blood on the floor.

Scarborough takes the tray from her: "The yarrow worked; she's going to be fine."

She wonders how the baby could have been so white, when Scarborough's skin is so dark, almost black, and Lucy's so golden brown; and she wonders whether Moses has wanted to have a baby sister.

The card Gloriana slipped in Charles Willson's waistcoat pocket slides up against the swell of his belly as he takes more coffee to face the day. *Thomas Cadwallader, Atty at Law* in fine script, and an address in the city. He recognizes the name, and remembers the man from his time in the Assembly. He understands what Gloriana meant: Thomas Cadwallader will know the laws that govern his household now, and may offer some guidance. *Lydia*, will he ever be free of thoughts of her? She came into his life before he knew there were choices to make.

Chapter 6

THE FARM A FEW MILES beyond the ridge has been stirring since before dawn, breakfast smoke rising from the
cabins and from the big house. The hoes are stacked by
the barn door and, as soon as it's full light, the men will begin
scraping the soil around the tobacco plants, trying to coax them
into health. Jefferson Randolph brought a thousand seeds with
him when his father, patience at an end, sent him from Virginia
with enough money to buy a farm far from home.

This morning, like most mornings, Jeff himself is still asleep,
snoring gently, still in his shirt and under-britches from the
night before. His handsome mouth lolls open, his eyelashes
flicker against his cheek. His wife, Arabella, is already in the
kitchen in her negligee, jiggling the baby, Jeremiah, against her
shoulder.

"Where's Anna?" she asks sharply of Bessie the cook, who
stirs the cornmeal mush without looking up. "Still at home, I
expect." She doesn't add the obligatory honorific, but Arabella is
too distracted to notice: "Well, send someone for her. The baby
won't suck."

Eva, the young girl sweeping in the corner, goes without a
word; a delay and the baby's screams could put them all under

the lash. Bessie moves the mush from fire to hearthstone, and turns to Arabella. "I can take him until Anna comes," she says, not unkindly, but again omitting to add *Ma'am*, until Arabella looks at her sharply, noticing now.

"Ma'am," she adds: an obvious afterthought, shading to mockery. Arabella decides not to take offense, handing the wriggling baby from her smooth white hands to Bessie's work-roughened brown ones. The baby, they're both aware, calms instantly. Arabella, to hide her embarrassment, begins to order the meals for the day: lunch for eight guests; dinner for ten visitors from Virginia who'll spend the night.

"We'll want oysters and game. Wild duck. Wild mushrooms. Vegetable terrines. Sally Lunn bread. Custards and berries; a Lady Baltimore cake."

"Ducks is nesting now, ma'am."

"All the easier to find them." The list is as demanding as she can make it, ending only at the limit of her imagination.

"And we'll need more servants at the table since Scarborough and Lucy are gone."

"I'll have to take some girls from the fields. . ." Bessie's voice trails off with the difficulty this day has brought.

Arabella waves her hand as if to wave away all impediment.

"Do whatever you need to do," she says, and startles to find Anna beside her: a young woman of her own age and height, with a sleeping brown baby, Jeremiah's size, on her shoulder.

"Are your nipples clean?" A careless glance at Anna's full bodice with the damp milk-spot on one side.

Anna has to tell herself not to react to such treatment. "Yes, ma'am." She hands her own child to Eva and takes Jeremiah from Bessie.

"Keep him all day and overnight. I have guests coming." Arabella turns with a swirl of muslin, bolstered by her ability to give orders. "And have the midday meal ready promptly at noon."

The woman and the girl in the kitchen don't speak after she's gone upstairs, but they don't need to; in their glances and gestures an abiding outrage is clear as they tend to the breakfast, the babies, the day's work. Scarborough and Lucy won't be easy to replace: Scar with his powdered wig and velvet livery greeting the guests, serving them, pouring the wines with authority, any hint of resistance carefully disguised, apparent only to keen eyes in the slight excess of his deference. Lucy with her light hand at biscuits and gift for the most delicate dishes, using recipes Thomas Jefferson's chef James Hemings himself brought from France.

"Antigua and Yarrow?" Anna suggests, "or someone from the Peales'?"

"The Peales don't have servants, except now, Lucy and Scar, but run," Bessie turns to Eva, "and see if at least Antigua will come."

Upstairs in the big bedroom, Jefferson stirs as Arabella bends over him, reaches out without opening his eyes, puts one large hand on the shadow where her nightgown dips between her breasts, and pulls her to him, tearing the thin cloth straight to the hem. A ripping sound: a rip too in the fabric of the morning: Arabella stifles a cry and begins to tremble, dropping to her knees on the bed beside him. She had been an untouched girl when they married, and has to pretend not to be shocked by Jefferson's sudden lunges and insistence on positions that hurt her back, her knees and sometimes her wrists, when he ties them to the bed-posts. "There's too much to do today. . ." she manages to say, before he pushes her face into the pillow.

"If it doesn't get done, just blame *them*. That old Bessie could use a whipping to get her going," he says, pushing up her nightgown.

When Arabella struggles up, holding the torn edges of her night-gown together, she turns to, and on, him: "Why did you have to sell Scarborough and Lucy anyway?"

"Don't you like our portrait?" he says in the wheedling tone she's come to hate.

Charles Willson's painting of them with a background of tobacco fields—flourishing in an optimistic projection—hangs in the dining room, presiding over every meal. It's often seemed to her a validation—the reason she's entitled to order everyone in the house to do her bidding; her consolation when Jefferson stays out drinking and losing at cards in town—but this morning she wishes it had never been, or that he'd been able to pay for it. "If only you hadn't lost so much as soon as the paint was dry," she says, drawing herself up with as much appearance of dig-nity as she can manage—rubbed raw on every soft surface —and unsteady on her feet.

Downstairs she yells instructions to everyone in sight; her par-ents have said they'll be there at noon. Bessie looks at her with an age-old skepticism that conveys without words how inept she is. A menu like this should have been planned weeks ahead; now they'll just have to make do.

"It's not the right time for hunting duck," she says, without the *ma'am*.

"Tell them to kill some chickens then," Arabella says crossly. "Do what you can." She's wanted to show her parents how well she can run a house, had wanted to please them so much that, lulled by the fine food and wine, they'll agree to the loan she plans to ask of them. Noticing Antigua and Yarrow, just arrived by cart, she asks Yarrow: "Do you know wine? Find the best the cellar has to offer." Not waiting for his reply, she hurries to tell the garden crew what vegetables to pick, what flowers.

———

The Davises are as prominent a family in Virginia as the Randolphs; when Jefferson and Arabella married it seemed the joining of two great planter dynasties.

The wedding was famously grand, thanks to two hundred enslaved workers—some borrowed from neighboring planta-tions—who cleaned for days, hunted and foraged and picked the freshest ingredients, cooked from James Hemings' French recipes, baked the local hams cured on plantation, fried chickens in black skillets, baked breads that were meltingly light, created a cake that was such a monument to culinary artistry that Arabella was hesitant to cut it. Jefferson had no such reluctance, plunging his grandfather's sword into the unresisting surface with a vigor that made the male guests laugh and the women hide their know-ing smiles behind their hands. They wouldn't know that on this wedding night the husband was so drunk his groomsmen had to drag him to bed; only the house staff knew, pulling the unstained bedsheets to wash them the next morning.

When the Davises arrive, in a coach and four, with trunks and servants enough for a month's stay—although they've planned to be there only a few days—the house is filled with flowers black hands have gathered and arranged—although Arabella has insisted on re-arranging a few of the most prominent bouquets. The furniture gleams with tallow; the food and wines are on hand, if not quite conforming to Arabella's menu. Yarrow serves with grace, if a bit uncertainly at first, not having done this work for years. At one point, after he has gone back into the pantry, Mrs. Davis leans across the table to Arabella, lowering her voice theatrically, not realizing or caring that several footmen stand against the walls, waiting to re-fill glasses and remove empty plates.

"What happened to Scarborough? He was so elegant."

For answer, Arabella looks pointedly at Jefferson, who lifts his glass: "Fine wine, isn't it? Left over from our wedding."

After dinner, Samuel Davis draws his daughter away before he takes cigars and liqueurs in the library with his son-in-law. "Where did Scarborough go?"

She has never lied before—except for the polite falsehoods that harm no one: complimenting a friend on her unbecoming new dress; telling her mother that everything is fine, even as Jefferson comes home later and later, more sodden with drink—but now she creates an untruth that will affect everyone around her: "Oh, he and Lucy ran away."

Her father stands a bit straighter, like the Revolutionary War captain he once was: "Runaways? There are remedies for that. We know how to take care of those things in Virginia."

"Oh, I don't think. . ." she starts to say, but Pandora's box, once opened, can't be so quickly shut.

"Give me some descriptions and I'll know how to find them."

This conversation has taken a direction different from the one she'd hoped for; she'll have to work quickly to bring it back: "Father, I wanted to ask you"—here she puts her hand on his arm—"The tobacco crop has been so poor, maybe because of the weather, maybe because the farmhands aren't working hard enough. . . ."

Samuel Davis considers: "You'll need a tougher overseer; that almost always does the trick. But right now: Do you need money?"

Her lies, once begun, become almost automatic; she looks surprised, as if money were the farthest thing from her mind: "Oh, I hadn't thought . . . But yes, we could always use some."

The next morning, after her parents' coach has driven away, Jefferson slaps her buttocks and laughs: "You did a good job, wench. They'll be glad to see me at the bank."

She can't resist: "Unless you gamble it all away," but says it half under her breath as he turns to berate the overseer waiting for the day's orders. "You'll be seeing your replacement any day." Which means the whip falls on every back; work days stretch past sunset; rations are cut in half.

Chapter 7

Samuel Davis considers the men before him—a word to his man Elijah has brought them: one taller, heavier, sunbrowned, his face lined but still handsome, carrying himself with an air of authority, of competence; the other slight, pale, with stubble at his chin and an involuntary smile.

"Gentlemen," Davis waves to two chairs set before his writing table. "I have a proposition for you."

The younger man grins and shifts forward in his chair; the older simply waits. It will take them a day to get ready; they'll leave at dusk and be in Pennsylvania by morning.

When they ride past the tobacco fields and up the Randolphs' drive, the men hoeing don't dare look—the overseer has brought his long whip today—but they hear the hoofbeats and know what's coming is nothing good. Arabella sees them from her bedroom window: a substantial man in a black hat with a pistol in his belt; a smaller man who doesn't merit her notice. She smooths back her hair; she has no time for powder or rouge, let alone a change of dress. Luckily, Jefferson has risen early for a change and ridden to town; the shipment of Madeira he's ordered has arrived in port, and he trusts no one but himself to bring it home.

The men scrape their boots with perfunctory politeness before the door. Eva, wide-eyed with alarm, has let them in and fled back to the kitchen.

"Ira Shaw, ma'am," the larger man says. "John Smith," the smaller one mumbles, and then, disturbingly, giggles. Arabella notices the iron ring of indenture around his throat.

"Can you give us a description, ma'am? A man and a woman, Mr. Davis said."

Arabella hasn't ever looked at Scarborough and Lucy long enough to describe them. He served her food and stood behind her chair at meals. Lucy was just a shape at the hearth. "A tall, thin man," she stays," and a small, thin woman."

"What color?"

"Black, of course." She's not used to so many questions. "Oh, he's very dark, and she's much lighter."

"Any scars or marks to tell them by?"

"I can't think of any." She's missed the scar at the base of Scarborough's neck, the brand.

"They took the boy with them."

Ira Shaw frowns; it's unusual enough that a couple would run away together, but that they would take a child along strains credulity. "How old?" he asks, but Arabella has no idea.

"We'll do what we can." Smith giggles into his hand. "When did you notice they were gone?"

Arabella rises to signal the interview's end. "My husband is out today, but I can give you . . ."

"Just coffee, ma'am. Your father paid us in full, in advance." Shaw wears his reputation like a perfectly cut coat.

In the kitchen, Bessie pours two cups of coffee from the pot on the hob without looking at Shaw and Smith. Shaw finds the coffee bitter, but compliments her anyway, in his dangerously soft voice: "Just what I needed," and asks without expecting her to answer: "Anything you can tell me about Scarborough and Lucy?"

He's pulled his purse casually out of his waistcoat pocket.

Bessie shakes her head without moving from the stew she's stirring. Smith takes a step towards her, but Shaw raises his hand to halt him.

Arabella, arranging flowers in the drawing room, watches them ride out toward the neighboring farm, proud to have set in motion such an act of worldly consequence, sure no one will care to discover her lie.

When Shaw and Smith ride through orchards to the farm where Antigua and Yarrow live, they find a pleasant landowner who simply shakes his head. He suggests they ask the Peales, who don't own slaves themselves but might have seen this family passing through. "They'll want to get north as fast as possible, I expect," he offers.

Mag opens the door to the peremptory knock and steps back, alarmed at their obvious guns and stern faces, so unlike most visitors to this house. Rubens, who was weeding the garden when they rode up, has come to stand just behind them. "Mr. Peale has gone to town on business," he says, surprising even Shaw, who's usually surprised by nothing. "My stepmother is ill; I'm Mr. Peale's son. How can I help you?"

When she hears Scarborough and Lucy's names, Mag runs to the kitchen, happy to be too insignificant to be noticed. Lucy is still in her room, recuperating; Peggy has never pushed her. Scarborough could be anywhere, but most likely is in the stable, currying the horses or cleaning tack. Without knowing why, she tells him to hide and not come out until she tells him to, waving her partial hand vaguely in the direction of the house. "Please!" she urges, and he obeys, understanding her fear without knowing its cause.

Later, Rubens will bring a basket of new beets to the kitchen to be cleaned of mud and boiled for lunch. "They were looking for Scarborough and Lucy, and for Moses, if they'd known his name.

I said I hadn't seen them, but it took them a while to believe me before they decided to go away. I was afraid Scarborough or Moses might come in at any moment. Those men mean nothing good." He, who barely speaks, is out of breath after this unaccustomed speech.

Mag finds Scarborough asleep on a hay bale in the old mare's stall. He looks up at her: "Thank you," and takes in his hand the hand no one ever touches.

Mag hardly ever thinks of her difference unless someone reminds her of it, as Peggy did when she first came, trying to be helpful, showing her how to wash the plates in a way that was awkwardly unhelpful. Angelica, watching, had said, "Peggy, I think Mag can figure out how to do things herself."

Peggy, who has lived with Peales almost all her life and knows the unspoken rules, didn't say she was afraid Mag would break something, and was more pleased than relieved when Mag proved her first thought wrong. She needs the help that Mag is eager to give; the girl has found that she loves working in the kitchen for the way plain, raw objects are changed through knives and fire and care.

Peggy is a plain cook, having eaten only the most meager food in a house where her mother was always exhausted and had no money for more than the cheapest ingredients. Potatoes mostly, and the vegetables the grocer couldn't sell, the rare bone the butcher let go for nothing. She has had to learn to cook the recipes that Charles Willson has brought from his visits to Monticello; has had, with Angelica's help, to translate his eccentric spelling into words that she with her rudimentary reading skill can recognize.

She values Mag's quiet attention, and sees that her partial hand is light with baking, her sense of taste acute. In the continuous work of the kitchen, Mag is entirely self-forgetful; when she's brought back to herself, usually by some visitor to the house—Mr.

Franklin or Eliza's parents—she's resentful, as if woken from a happy dream. Mr. Franklin has told her, repeatedly: "Perseverance is the most important thing," and given her a gold coin, as if she were still begging on the street. The DePeysters say nothing when she serves them, but look as if the sight of her offends them.

Here in the horse stall, she doesn't pull her hand away. She's aware without being told that she's done something important: an awareness confirmed by Charles Willson's voice calling from the house: "Scarborough, are you out there?" with unmistakable urgency. He's just come back from the city, having taken Moses with him. He's found the boy so quick to learn, he wants to show him the larger world, in this case, a lawyer's office, where he's gone to learn what laws Pennsylvania has passed since his years in the Assembly, when the bill to abolish slavery failed.

Moses had sat in the city office, watching and listening to the large white men talking and smoking their pipes. Charles Willson took notes with his quill, covering the foolscap with his fast-running script, nodding to the boy to collect the pages as they leave his hand. "You won't want to learn to spell from me, but you can figure out what we've talked about from reading these," he said to Moses when they'd repaired to a tavern nearby.

Coming from full sun into the hall, with Scarborough behind her, Mag blinks at Charles Willson in the dark hall. He's quite a large man, but not so large that the sight of him should surprise as it always does. He says to Scarborough without preamble: "Do you think your wife is well enough to come downstairs? I need to talk to you both. And to Moses."

Mag knows how to disappear unnoticed; in the kitchen she finds Moses eating a thick slice of fresh bread laden with butter. He looks up at her over a smooth golden surface that almost reflects his face. She looks back, and there is in both of them a delight: between them, a spark almost like the electricity Mr. Franklin says he can bring down from the sky, before they each shyly look down or away.

In the drawing room with its mirrors and formal sofas, inherited from Rachel's family, Charles Willson gestures to Lucy and Scarborough to sit opposite him. "Moses, please bring my box of papers, and sit with your parents."

Lucy sits very straight with obvious effort next to Scarborough, who presses her hand reassuringly, although he has no power to reassure, let alone protect her. He wonders what this strange white man, who has asked if he likes horses and given him the run of the stables, has thought up next.

"I don't want to keep you," Charles Willson begins, but at the look of terror on both of their faces, Lucy's crumpling with silent tears, changes direction: "No, no, I don't mean *not* to keep you here"—he hesitates to say the word *enslaved*—and goes on: "I mean to free you." Lucy slumps against Scarborough, who tightens his arm around her. "The Emancipation Statute says that all free men and women have to be able to earn a living. That means indentured servants too," he adds irrelevantly, guiltily. "So we'll need to make sure you can do that before I can, as the law says, *manumit* you. Lucy, you know kitchens?" Lucy nods, bewildered that she's being asked something. Scarborough grimaces, and Charles Willson guesses: "You're good with horses?"

"And our boy?" Scarborough brings himself to ask, as Lucy stiffens beside him, bracing for this white man's decision. She can't imagine that they have come so far—all the years pretending that the young Randolph pleased her with his sour tongue and short stub of a penis rooting in her—*to have come this far* to have their son torn from them, as she was torn from her mother.

Charles Willson motions to Moses to bring the box with his papers, and rummages through them. "I can't find the exact place, but the law in this state says a young person"—he omits *slave* from the text here—"can't be freed until he or she is twenty-six years old. So Moses can live here with us until then and learn to do whatever best suits him."

"And where will we go?" Lucy manages to ask through the terror in her throat, thinking: *Of course, he's found a way to trick and torment us.*

"Wherever you want," Charles Willson begins, before seeing what he hasn't understood. "Close by. There will be work for you in the neighborhood."

"Doing what?" Scarborough asks, with a bluntness that only increases Lucy's terror. He hasn't answered when Charles Willson asked if they "knew kitchens."

He's known the dining room all too well: carrying the heavy platters from the kitchen to the main house, bowing as he served each oblivious white person, wearing over his shaved head the powdered wig whose tail scratched his neck and hid the brand there. On any other plantation, he would have been in the tobacco field, but since Jefferson had noticed Lucy, and knowing that this household was the end of the line before he'd be sold south, he practiced being a butler with an ironic pride in following the rules borrowed from England and teaching them to the footmen.

If Charles Willson is startled by Scarborough's directness, he's also relieved; perhaps they can talk, man to man. "You'll need to do something no one else does, or does as well. You'll need to be in demand." He's as direct as the man before him: practical and blunt, having made his own way in places where no one knew him, but understanding the stakes are different for each of them.

"Two bounty hunters came by here today," he says. "I'm not sure why, since you haven't run."

The gratitude Scarborough feels is the same as when Mag came to the horse stall to tell him the men looking for him and Lucy had gone. Tears, embarrassingly for this man proud of his strength, well and spill over; Charles Willson chooses to ignore them. Something has changed between them: a degree of trust unimaginable a few days or centuries before.

"I could teach you my craft," he begins. Scarborough is startled; he hasn't envisioned learning to paint. "I mean, what I started with: saddles and bridles, leather and metal work. A man may need only one saddle in his lifetime, but stirrup straps and bridles always need mending. No one around here took up where I stopped; the nearest saddlers are in the city."

Born into slavery, Scarborough has chosen nothing. He merely nods in agreement; the dozen questions in his mind stay there.

Charles Willson gathers his papers together and turns to Lucy. "How are you?"

He looks over his glasses in a way no white man looks at her: not calculating her potential as a worker or mentally undressing her. She hesitates a long, uncomfortable moment, and Scar says, "She needs a few days' more rest."

Blood has stained her underclothes every day since the stillbirth. Her color, usually a rich brown, has paled. If the bleeding would stop, she might be able to forget the way her body has betrayed her. If she could work, her mind could move past Jefferson's sodden body on hers.

"I'll be better soon," she surprises them, and herself, her low voice strong.

Chapter 8

WHEN LUCY COMES DOWN to the kitchen days later, Peggy looks at her sharply but takes her at her word: "I'm fine," she insists, although she's still pale and holds the table-edge to steady herself. Peggy grasps that she's only barely there. Peggy, who lost all her children within months of their births, suggests that vegetables are best cut by someone sitting: There are new onions and carrots to be chopped, and lettuce leaves to be separated from their heads and washed.

Lucy cuts the carrots into ovals and breaks the lettuce gently. She asks how the onions and carrots are to be used; Moses is turning a leg of lamb on the spit outside. Peggy is used to the simplest ways of cooking, the most meager meals; she's surprised by Lucy's delicate knife-work and her questions about garlic and mint. "I worked with James at Monticello for a few months," Lucy almost apologizes, realizing as she says this that the name of Thomas Jefferson's chef means nothing to Peggy and the girls. "Do you have a kitchen garden?"

Peggy shows her the walled plot Charles Willson has cultivated on the south side of the house, where she finds thyme and lavender, spikes of tarragon, and, in the shadiest spot, the mint she hoped for. The garlic will need planting in the fall.

"May I?" Lucy shows Mag how to strip the mint leaves from their stems, and then how to chop them fine without crushing them. "Do you have a whetstone? Moses could sharpen this knife."

Peggy is so relieved to be helped and so aware of the other woman's greater skill that she steps back gratefully; turning to the potatoes waiting for her in the metal sink, she pumps the shining stream of water over them, scrubbing each one in her large hands. When Rubens comes into the kitchen with his hat full of beets, Peggy turns to Lucy: "What should we do with them?'

"Vinegar, and do we have oil?" Peggy looks blank. "Or butter then." And with Lucy's question to Rubens: "Do you know anyone who grows garlic?" it's clear who will run the kitchen now.

Charles Willson wants his food fresh and plentiful, which is why he bought this land to farm. He notices the subtle changes in the meals: at first, slight seasonings that brighten the flavors of simple vegetables. As the season moves toward high summer, Lucy has procured, with Rubens' help, more exotic herbs and spices. Definite bursts of taste make him sit up straight and make Eliza wrinkle her nose. Of squash baked with a hint of curry that even Margaret Peale devours, she complains: "This makes my throat hurt" and calls for more spring water.

When she feels well enough—this first pregnancy is hard on her—Eliza visits the kitchen, raising lids, poking into pots, tasting a just-baked roll. Peggy is pleasant but wary; although she knows that Charles Willson has the final say on everything in this house, Eliza's displeasure can hurt everyone. Lucy doesn't look up, as if not looking at Eliza will keep her from being noticed. She's showing Mag how to pinch off a chunk of dough from the mass she's just kneaded and shape it into a roll, when Eliza interrupts: "How can that girl do anything? There's no point in teaching *her.*"

Mag flushes with shame, as if her birth was her fault, but Peggy says sharply: "She's been doing just fine," and Eliza turns to taste the vegetable soup, eager to complain: "What's *in* this?"

"Just garlic and rosemary, ma'am. Would you like me to take some out and add water to it for you?" Lucy asks.

Eliza, too outclassed to answer, turns away and leaves the kitchen with a flounce of her skirts. It can't be easy coming into this household where she must live in the shadow of another woman who was first love, wife, mother, daughter of all the people still here mourning her loss, but Eliza's nature makes her life even harder. She has always had every material thing her father could buy, and his buying power was vast in the early days of Old New York. Modesty, generosity and good humor are qualities she only seemed to have when Charles Willson courted her a year after Rachel's death. Margaret Peale and Peggy will agree, nights when Peggy pulls the old woman's stockings from her swollen feet: Charles Willson was too hasty to replace Rachel and is blind to how hard it must be for Eliza to have landed in this house, expected to be wife, mother, and mistress. Peggy, who does the laundry, says it's especially hard, since she arrived "as a green virgin."

"And," Margaret will invariably add tartly: "none too nice besides." The two of them will share a laugh as Peggy rubs Margaret's purplish old feet before blowing out their lamp.

In the kitchen, Mag has stopped pinching the dough and steps back, not wanting her tears to spoil the rolls and not wanting Peggy and Lucy to see her shame. The two women share a glance before Peggy touches Mag's shoulder: "Don't let her bother you. We need to get these rolls in the oven if they're going to be done by lunch." Grateful, Mag turns back to her favorite task: patting the round shapes into tin forms; she loves the way the dough springs back at her touch, as if it's alive.

Moses is at the kitchen door, carrying the roasted lamb before him, unable to open the door or knock, and trained not to raise his voice. Mag, who's always aware of his presence, wipes her hands on her apron. "Coming," she calls, almost sings.

When he sees her, his face, which has been knotted in concentration, transforms to delight. "I'm about to drop this,' he says, as if making a great joke. "Can't have that," Mag answers, her delight in seeing him matching his in seeing her. When they have a free moment, after morning lessons in reading, writing, and drawing, and in the brief recess before chores begin, they find ways to tease each other: Moses snatching her hair bow, Mag simply touching his back and running off with a "Touch you last!"

Angelica and Isba watch them, amused, but don't try to join in, feeling themselves too grown up for such childish games. Peggy and Lucy exchange glances when Mag and Moses rush through the kitchen; it's as if a magnet were attached to each of them, drawing them together. Charles Willson, too, has noticed the current that runs between them; he's already begun to wonder what the future holds for them, and in what ways he can guide them. Rubens, who's always quiet, becomes quieter, even moody, when he sees them; once he yelled as they ran through the just-weeded lettuce: "Stay out of my garden!"

Two slight bumps have begun to rise on Mag's shirtwaist, now that she's turned twelve. Peggy has talked to her about what to do when the blood comes down between her legs, shows her how to make pads out of torn sheets to tie around herself, although Mag tosses her head, as if she can't be bothered. Her face has begun to lose its childish roundness; her cheekbones have begun to give her an adult elegance that Rembrandt and Raphaelle, training to be artists of such faces, have noticed. And Rubens, intent on his gardening, would never admit that he has noticed too, but if asked in some confessional to reveal what he feels, would talk about the red in her hair in sunlight, when she runs laughing through his well-tended plants.

The youngest brother, Titian, who loves to draw the wildlife he catches around the farm, thinks Mag's partial hand looks like the nose of a star-nosed mole: flexible and strange. He tries hard to hide his fascination and wants to draw her, but she notices him looking—can *feel* a stare, she'd say, if asked—and stares back, daring him to speak until he blushes and pretends to be examining something else.

Chapter 9

HALF ON THE FARM—where Eliza gives birth to the child they name Linnaeus—half in the city painting or building his museum, anyone less focused than Charles Willson coming into the Northeast Square at midday would be stopped by the scent of roasting meats on the little braziers, let alone the sight of jugglers, fire-eaters, and stilt-walkers; or be slowed by the sound of fiddle and flute, and even would join in the dancing. But he, with one object in mind, has hurried halfway down a side street when he realizes Moses isn't behind him.

"Are you hungry?" He's already pulled out his purse, but the boy doesn't answer, too absorbed to hear or to feel hunger. The girl Moses is watching holds a board in front of her between both knees. She bends to it with a pencil in her teeth, occasionally brushing her paper with a toe or pushing back her hair with her ankle.

One foot pokes from her skirts; it's small, with only three toes, and bare, although the spring air has an edge of cold.

Charles Willson reflexively drops some coins into the basket in front of her and is about to move on, but Moses tugs at his sleeve. The girl smiles her thanks around the pencil, and fixes both man and boy with a clear, unembarrassed gaze that causes

Charles Willson to look at the paper she holds so skillfully: petals and branches flow from her mouth as they might from his hand.

"Do you sell your work, Miss?" he asks.

She lowers the pencil carefully into the valley of her skirts. She positions the pencil so her mouth can pick it up again and says, in a woman's voice, deeper and stronger than he's expected: "Of course. This isn't quite finished, but there are others that are." She gestures with her head to a row of images behind her, guarded by a younger girl: flowers seen and not seen on earth, their centers formed by tiny letters that begin: *The Lord is my shepherd. . . .*

"I'll take this one for my museum; is this enough?" He holds out an unlikely sum in his palm. Moses' surprise comes less from the amount Charles Willson is offering than the fact that there *is* currently no museum. "Well, for my museum when it's open."

"Much more than enough," she answers, and empties all the coins into the basket by her feet. He takes note of the name in round script in the margin of the drawing: *Martha Ann Honeywell.* "My pleasure, Miss Honeywell," he says. "And thank my man Moses for paying attention."

She nods to Moses, taking up her pencil again with an unself-conscious grace he's seen in Mag, and taking him in: a slim boy with skin the color of polished maple, whose large hands and long arms predict his adult height.

As he follows Charles Willson, carrying the board that holds her drawing, he hears another passer-by say to her: "How do you do that? If I were you, I'd stay home in bed," and hears Martha Ann's answer, "I do God's work."

Chapter 10

S O VEGETABLES CAN GROW and be harvested all year, Charles
Willson has decided that the farm needs a greenhouse; he's
written to Thomas Jefferson for advice, and Jefferson has
sent his builder's plans. "He also sent seeds: French filet beans
and English peas." Charles Willson tosses the packets across the
table to Rubens. "Of course, his builder is his son and also his
slave, and his crew of hundreds will work day and night until
the job is done. They don't have a choice. With just the four, five,
six of you"—he looks around the table at Rembrandt, Raphaelle,
Rubens, and Titian, then at Scarborough and Moses—"and seven
with me, we'll get it done."

Rubens is eager, Titian agreeable; Scarborough keeps his
eyes on his plate, knowing he has no choice of assignments, and
Moses looks at Charles Willson in wonder. No white man he's
ever heard, or heard of, has talked this way, and no white family
would have urged him to sit with them at meals: something Lucy
has tried to avoid by making herself busy in the kitchen, bringing out dishes, and slipping into her seat only when all the food
has been brought to table. She doesn't know what to say to any
of them: the boys and Charles Willson sharing the news of the
neighborhood; Angelica tending to baby Linneaus; Isba teasing

her brothers for their table manners; their grandmother murmuring compliments and complaints. Eliza watches how she uses her fork and knife, as if assuming she doesn't know how to use them. One of the hardest parts of life here for her is having to act as if she and her family are just like the white people.

This day Charles Willson has another announcement: his nephew Charlie, his dead sister's boy, will be coming to live with them. "He's just your age," Charles Willson nods at Mag and Moses, "and he's lost both his parents." He doesn't add, *Be nice to him.* The rules of the house are few, set by example and unspoken.

Charlie comes on the Philadelphia stage on a day when rain pours off his oilskin coat and wide-brimmed hat. He is silent, stunned, and unsmiling as his uncle introduces him to the cousins he's never met, with their strange, un-English names; the girl who has something wrong with her hand; a brown-skinned boy his height. An older woman helps him shrug out of his dripping coat and takes his hat. "I'm Peggy," she says brusquely but not unkindly, before telling one of the older boys to show him to an empty bedroom upstairs.

He grips his small valise tight and refuses Rembrandt's offer of help. He'd die before he'd expose its contents to this tall, confident cousin: the locket with his mother's picture and a curl of her hair; the shameful rag doll he's slept with all his life. His new bedroom is one of those under the deep eaves; he drops to the narrow bed under the single window and falls asleep without taking off his jacket and boots.

Rembrandt steps back and closes the door behind him, knowing what it is to lose one's mother: the blank space in the house, in the household's life, that all the activity on the farm, and the work of an artist's family, can't fill. How every day was full yet empty. But he, he thinks as he goes downstairs, has never been in a strange place, only here in the familiar one, where his father tries to distract his children and himself with new projects: planting, building, painting, and lessons, to prepare for a trip to Paris. Of course, his father would disappear after many dinners; Rembrandt would hear his horse coming back in the night and was old enough to be wise to his father's habits.

Now Charles Willson reminds them all to be kind to Charlie, insulting the oldest boys, who don't think they need to be told the obvious. Rembrandt and Raphaelle keep their heads down and their hands in their pockets; Titian cradles a baby woodchuck: a delicate fluff that gives no hint of the rapacious adult to come; Rubens cleans his muddy fingernails with his pocket knife. The girls and Moses follow Charles Willson's every word.

He hasn't, however, thought to remind Charlie about kindness. When the newcomer sits down to the lunch-time meal, he refuses the soup with a wrinkled nose and demands that Lucy bring him something else: "There's no cold beef or salmon?" When she simply shakes her head without addressing him, he angrily pulls off a chunk of bread and leaves the table, scattering crumbs behind him. Charles Willson shakes his head when Peggy rises to follow him: "Leave him for a while."

The "while" lasts a week, during which Charlie orders Moses to pick up his clothes and draw his bath: "Boy, I'll tell your master, my uncle, on you. . . ." He has questioned Mag with accusatory anger, as if her lack of knowledge about her hand is a deliberate failing: "Why don't you know what happened? Does your mother have ugly hands, too?" And when Mag replies that she's never known her mother, Charlie says: "I'll bet she wished you had never been born," at which Mag, who has been determined to resist Charlie's aggressions, and is trying to obey Charles Willson's directions, flees in tears.

Charlie tries to flatter Angelica and Isba, admiring their clothes and hair; he keeps an admiring distance from their older brothers. He is careful not to offend Peggy, who he sees is a power in this house and, after his first demand of Lucy, avoids making another. But when he goes to the stable one morning and orders Scarborough, "Saddle me the best horse, boy," the "while" is stretched to breaking.

Scarborough answers respectfully, although he refuses to say the obligatory *young master*: "The best horse is reserved for your uncle" and continues to curry the gelding's shining coat. At which Charlie grabs the shovel leaning by the stable door and swings it furiously at Scarborough's back: "Bring it, boy!" Charlie is so small that the shovel can't reach the tall man's head, and he's too weak to do as much harm as he hopes. Struck across the back, Scarborough staggers against the horse, who has never been tied in the stall and bolts into the stable yard in terror and clatters into the road.

Charles Willson, who has just come out of the house with his painting case, begins to yell: "Bonnie Prince! Bonnie Prince!" at the horse, who turns his head a moment before running on. Scarborough is on his knees, expecting that Charlie will swing again. "Sir! Charles Willson!" he cries, sure he won't be heard, but desperate: "Sir!" Which is enough to scare Charlie, who runs behind the stable, flinging the shovel behind him.

When his uncle finds him, after Bonnie Prince has slowed to a walk and been led home by Rubens, who caught sight of him through the garden hedge, Charlie is sitting on the ground, arms around his knees, out of breath from crying.

"Is your horse all right?" he manages to ask Charles Willson when his uncle kneels beside him and brings out his handkerchief for Charlie's wet face. A woman would have smoothed the hair back from the boy's forehead, but Charles Willson hates to condescend. "I was your age when my father died," he begins to talk of those days: his mother's grief and the terrible need to keep everyone fed. How he was bound out to a saddle-maker and had to get hides from the slaughterhouse: "I scraped off the fur," he says, and then: "Charlie, you haven't asked how Scarborough is."

"I thought he was your slave," the boy answers, bewildered.

"And not a human being?" asks his uncle, who has drawn back from him, from the intimacy of telling his life story. "At Belfield, you have a lot to learn."

Later that day, after Charles Willson has left for the city, the dogs rush out, both vying to be the fiercest defender of their home, as a trap turns in at the drive and pulls up at the door. Mag, washing a stairwell window, sees the occupants freeze in place: a boy at the reins; a womanly shape beside him; a puff of skirt, more than a girl, behind them.

"Yes?" she calls from the half-opened door, calling sternly "Argus!" to the old dog, "Apollo!" to the new stray.

"This is Mr. Peale's farm?" the woman asks, climbing down at Mag's nod, bringing with her a basket holding an empty glass jar. Perennial worry has etched furrows between her eyes, whether she's consciously frowning or not, but she seems closer to Eliza's age than to Charles Willson's. Young-ish, Mag thinks, although she pays more attention to the puff of muslin still in the trap; and the bare leg sticking from it, with, it seems, three curved toes at its end. "Can I help you?"

"I've heard you keep bees and might sell some wax." The woman's frown deepens: "It's for my daughter: the ends of her bones..." The puff behind her leans forward, speaks: "Beeswax is the best way to keep the skin from cracking." Mag sees that both legs end in bone; they're shaped like Lucy's maple rolling pin, tapering at the ends. The voice is firm and full of music: "I'm Martha Ann Honeywell; this is my mother, Mariah, and my brother, Josiah."

Martha Ann's face is oval, her eyes eloquent, the bits of hair Mag can see under her cap laced with gold glints. "I'll show you the way to the bee house. Tell Rubens I sent you," she says, taking on an unaccustomed authority that matches Martha Ann's. She can see that the ends of those limbs are red; it's hard to look at them without wincing. She runs ahead of the trap down the farm lane toward the bee house as Josiah drives the trap slowly behind her.

Chapter 11

THE LEATHER-WORKING TOOLS ARE CLEAN, safely tied in their leather roll, but the frame on which saddles are built is covered with hay dust when Charles Willson takes it from the tack-room shelf. He begins to sneeze in short explosions; Scarborough, leaning against the door-frame, offers: "God bless," at which Charles Willson, convulsed by another sneeze, waves his hand in dismissal. When he manages to speak, he explains, "You'd have to say it a hundred times, so thank you, but don't bother," and is lost in another explosion. Scarborough takes the saddle-tree from him into the yard, where he begins to wipe it clean with a polishing cloth.

When he comes back to himself, Charles Willson says, "I can show you better out here," and puts the saddle-tree on the wide stone wall. "The leather goes over it?" Scarborough asks; he's always wondered how this was done. Charles Willson nods. "We'll need more leather than we have here. I'll stop by the tannery when I'm in town." He's relieved not to have to expose his rusty skills to this tall, watchful man, who, he suspects, will understand how to build a saddle faster than he can show him. There's something wrong, he thinks, about teaching a grown man something he himself learned as a boy.

He never lacks reasons to go to town; today, besides leather, he needs new brushes and canvas; some tubes of paint have dried. He thinks to take Moses with him, but the skins will be heavy. Remembering the strange men who stopped at the house just a week ago, he senses, without knowing exactly what they wanted, that it's not safe to take Scarborough.

He arrives at Gloriana's in the middle of the day, stepping over a pail of soapy water on the steps. Marcus, the door-keeper, opens to his knock, in shirtsleeves and work pants; his wiry hair swings in a braid, free of the wig. He tries to hide his surprise:

"Mr. Peale! Was Miss Glory expecting you?"

Holding the neck of her negligee, Gloriana herself is behind him. She moves towards Charles Willson, stretching out her hands: "Charles Willson, is anything wrong?" Doors close in the hallway above them; there's a burst of quickly stifled laughter.

He has never seen her without her powder and rouge or the black beauty mark above her lip. Her red, gray-streaked hair looks as it does, unbound, in bed, but today, with the sun flickering against the carpet, he's not thinking of bed.

"So," she begins, facing him over coffee in her room, "it makes you uncomfortable to tell a Black man what to do? What about the people you sold when your committee took the Tory estates?"

"I was following the law," he answers, more uncomfortable than before.

"There were families who had lived on those estates for years; they were broken apart in those sales. Do you know where they went? Cotton fields, rice fields, tobacco. Do you know what their lives were like?"

He holds up his hand to stop her, and she takes pity on him. "On another subject, there's a Slave Patrol around: a big sun-tanned white man named Ira, and one who says his name is John. He roughed up one of my girls the other night. He has the iron ring around his neck, and giggles all the time." She shudders. "I had to tell Marcus to bar the door to him. The other wasn't so bad." Charles Willson looks at her sharply: "Not so bad" usually means she found a man attractive. She tosses her head, as if to dismiss the suspicion, and goes on: "They're looking for a family escaped from the Randolphs, who might be Scarborough and Lucy and the boy."

"But that fool Jefferson *gave* them to me."

"Tell that to the Slave Patrol and you'll get nowhere. Best hide them as well as you can, as I hide runaways here."

"Or free them," Charles Willson answers, anticipating what she'll say next.

"If they can make a living," she throws back his usual argument.

He kisses her cheek before he leaves, but holds both her hands tight and looks at her for a long moment, hoping to convey what he can't say. If he was asked, *Who is your best friend?* he wouldn't answer, Tom Jefferson or John Beale Bordley, but her. "I want to paint you," he says.

She simply shakes her head, and pushes him gently out the door.

In a room above a tavern in Sugar Alley, Jeb-who-goes-by "John Smith" is cleaning his pistol. "After I put it in her, it needs a good wipe-down." He giggles, and Ira Shaw simply grunts, which might mean anything but here indicates his deep disgust. He thinks of himself as a professional, and wonders how he allowed himself to be saddled with this idiot. *The money was good* is the answer he always gives himself.

"I'd like to go back there. She screamed like she was really hurt."

"I don't think they'll let you in again," Ira says, then realizes that resistance will make Jeb more eager. "It's too expensive any-way." He's pleased to come up with a compelling reason, knowing they'd be arrested if Jeb tried to push his way in, and wanting nothing to spoil this deal.

He tries a sure distraction: "There was something funny out there at that farm. We better go back."

Downstairs the two men find a large, well-dressed man at the bar, downing a glass of clear amber liquid. He glances at them sharply as he turns to go; the bar-keep, pulling a handful of coins across the bar towards himself, calls after him: "Don't stay a stranger, Mr. Peale."

The large man waves a hand in his direction, but doesn't turn.

"What arrogant fuck was that?" Jeb asks. Charles Willson hears the Scotch-Virginian burr from the doorway: a sound so soft when friendly, so menacing when not, and realizes this must be the Slave Patrol Gloriana mentioned.

"What'll you have?" the bar-keep asks, not answering the question.

A couple of working men slide into neighboring seats at the bar, and Jeb accosts them: "Would you like to hear how we do them slaves when we bring them in?" he giggles. The man nearest him turns a sweat-stained shoulder to him, and orders his drink. Jeb shrugs, sucks on his ale; Ira sees that this day's work is done before it started. He plans to make an early start on the next one, though.

The bar-keep pulls Ira aside when he and Jeb rise to go: "Don't bring your business here, if you know what's good for you." Ira nods, furious with the animal beside him.

Chapter 12

HURRYING HOME, Charles Willson flicks the whip over the horses' backs, more for the sound than the blow; he's brought the wagon for the heavy hides. Argus and the young Apollo bark and leap toward the tantalizing smells; Rubens and Scarborough don't have to be called to help unload the wagon. Rembrandt and Raphaelle slouch into the yard reluctantly. The older girls don't stir from their sewing, but Moses grabs a ragged edge of hide to seem helpful, even as Rembrandt sneers. Mag simply watches from the door as the glossy sheets—burnt umber, chestnut, deep black—are wrestled to the stable, where Charles Willson will show Scarborough how to shape them to the saddle-tree.

Dinner that night is roast lamb with the first carrots, potatoes, and peas that Rubens has brought in for Lucy, Mag and Peggy to wash, peel, shell, or shape.

Lucy has made rolls so light they seem to float out of their basket; Mag has chopped the herbs and washed and torn the lettuce into small, ruffled bites.

The evening light stays for hours at this time of year: golden across the family table, where Margaret Peale leans forward in her wheeled chair at one end and Charles Willson sharpens the carving knife over the roast at the other. Beside him, Eliza has left her bedroom for her first dinner in days; Peggy has been bringing her meals and taking the plates back untouched.

"This is perfectly delicious!" Eliza announces with a forced gaiety that makes her husband wince. "Peggy, I didn't know you could make everything taste so good—and these rolls!"

Peggy, who is used to Eliza's subtle and not-so-subtle jibes, and refuses to take offense, says mildly, "Lucy made the rolls." Lucy, who has slipped into her place next to Scarborough after bringing in the food, tries to make herself seem smaller, hoping Eliza won't go further. Eliza, though, waves her wine glass in Lucy's direction: "Your baking is magnificent! We should have a party."

Charles Willson looks sharply at her wine glass. He doesn't remember filling it or seeing her take the decanter. He tries not to show alarm; he prides himself on the high quality of his attention, and his ability to control—or guide, as he would insist—everyone under his protection.

Eliza waves her glass again, the wine sloshing over the rim. "Lucy and Scarborough, you can serve as you did at the Randolphs'." Lucy stiffens in her place; Scarborough grips his fork so hard the blood leaves his knuckles.

Charles Willson doesn't miss this; he bends close to Eliza, speaking almost under his breath against her powdered neck, as if preparing to seduce her: "We should go upstairs, my dear," and then places a hand against the small of her back and rises from the table, drawing her to him with an arm tight around her waist, almost dancing out the door. Those left in the room can hear the stumbling of their unsteady weight on the stairs.

Margaret Peale purses her lips in disapproval; she never expected that her son would marry so soon after Rachel died—and would marry *this*. If Charles Willson had asked her advice—but he asked no one, and now no one dares question his judgment. The oldest boys mock him and their stepmother; Raphaelle draws pornographic cartoons that imagine his father with unbuttoned britches, trying to find Eliza's negligible breasts and her unwelcoming thighs. Rembrandt will only laugh and act as if he's forgotten his mother; Rubens will turn crimson and turn away. Titian will come with a robin's nest and a bright blue egg, and begin to draw them. Peggy will frown and urgently give orders that don't need urgency.

This evening, Charles Willson returns to the table without embarrassment, ignoring the ripple of amusement from the boys' end of the table, although he notes it and the fact that they're becoming young men. He claps his hands, as full of false cheer as Eliza had been, but more convincing. "Yes, we'll have a feast and invite friends. Everyone will have work to do." He looks over at Margaret Peale: "Mother, may we use your dessert plates?" She nods graciously, unable to resist; these are fine old porcelain, painted with still lifes of fruits and vegetables, that Charles Willson, and especially James, admire: shockingly realistic in degrees of ripeness and mended with metal rivets. They're brought out on special occasions; only Peggy is trusted to wash them, and has never yet broken one.

Charles Willson hasn't forgotten how Lucy and Scarborough looked when asked to serve at table: "It'll be a buffet: this table and the sideboard piled high with food, and small tables where guests can sit to eat. We can plan the menu tomorrow. Peggy, Lucy and Rubens, you can decide what the food will be: what's best in the garden, what you'd like to make."

Of course, Eliza will have ideas of her own, will want delicacies from town and servants in livery, but Peggy tells her kitchen crew to persevere: "She'll never come in to help or see what we're doing. By the time it's on the table and guests are here, she won't say a word."

Guests are another point of difference. No one argues over

Dr. Franklin, but whether to ask the saddle-maker who's tutoring Scarborough, or the storekeeper who imports brushes and paints, or the small farmer just past the Randolphs' becomes the subject of barely muffled arguments when Charles Willson and Eliza retire to their rooms. The idea of inviting all the neighbors isn't what Eliza had in mind, and a buffet seems to her impossibly untidy. More than one evening, Charles Willson flings on the clothes he's just pulled off and leaves for town. Gloriana never argues, simply dismisses whoever is with her and sits smiling slightly, quizzically, her hair and skin dusted with gold in the oil lamp's light. "You're here often. Is Eliza pregnant again?" she says, hardly as a question.

All the candelabras have been found and now are lit, flickering a little in the breeze that comes off the meadows into the dining room through the open French doors. The guests have helped themselves from the table crowded with dishes—ham in rosy slices, pearly new potatoes, shining peas, ruffles of lettuce, mounds of napkin-covered biscuits—and find their names in Angelica's fine round hand on place-cards on the small tables here and on the terrace.

Peggy lets out the breath she hasn't realized she's been holding, and pushes her aunt to her place close to the big table. Rubens is proud of what he's grown but is sure no one has noticed its quality. Isba tries to call attention to the flowers, which she's arranged in bouquets—sweet pea blossoms and blousy peonies—and ends by tipping over one vase, creating a rush for rags and a fresh tablecloth. The silver she, Angelica, and Mag have polished gleams at each place, reflecting the candlelight and the women's bright dresses as they turn uncertainly, looking for their names.

Charles Willson has arranged the place-cards with a certain sense of mischief: the high-born landowner next to the artisan; the judge next to the wine merchant, but he refrains from causing painful confrontations, although some possibilities have crossed his mind. Lucy, for instance, can slip into her place near the kitchen door at a table with Moses, Mag, Peggy, and Grandmother Peale. But not before Jefferson Randolph has caught sight of her: "Lucy, my girl, how is my friend Charles Willson treating you? Has you well-dressed, I see."

Frozen in her seat, fork in hand, Lucy drops her head, wishing she could fall through the floor. But Jeff persists: "And where's that rapscallion husband—if we can call him that—of yours? Charles keeping him in line, I hope." He signals to Rembrandt to pour him another glass, although he's barely finished the first.

Across the room, Arabella has her own reasons for freezing in place; after a moment's pause, she tosses her powdered curls and touches her dinner partner: "And what fascinating project are you working on now, Dr. Franklin?" Everyone at that table, and the next, listens intently to what he says, as she knows they will.

Eliza, at the head of the largest table, is filled with dismay. When she suggested a party, this lack of order, as she sees it, of elegance, isn't what she had in mind. She envisioned not just the best silver and china on the table, but one long table, served by the slaves they have now—*Why not use them?* she'd asked Charles Willson more than once—and for guests, only people she calls *the best*. The food seems too plain, too close to its origins: the carrots and potatoes not the carefully manicured shapes she remembers from parties in New York; the sauces too simple.

She pokes her fork into the bright shards of parsley in the melted butter coating her potatoes, and flicks them to the edge of her plate. Why couldn't they have done better than this, have *out*done themselves?

She looks down the long table at Charles Willson, whose face is flushed with the food and wine; he seems perfectly content, even jubilant. For the first time in their married life, he disgusts her, wiping his lips with her best damask napkin and raising his glass to her with what she recognizes is a mocking smile. She coughs into her hand to hide what her expression must betray.

Rembrandt and Raphaelle refill the wine glasses with the attentiveness of experienced waiters; Angelica, Isba, and Mag remove the emptied plates from the correct side, as Peggy has taught them. Eliza holds her breath as Mag pulls her plate from the table, balancing it with both good and partial hands, and can't stop herself from saying: "I didn't think you could do that without dropping it."

Mag flushes and clenches her teeth, more angry than hurt. Charles Willson, who misses little, sets his glass down so hard that some wine leaps onto the virgin cloth, but, not to ruin the spirit of the evening, asks as she's heading into the kitchen: "What did you and Lucy make for dessert, Mag?"

"Wait and see," she says, with a familiarity that annoys Eliza, who has thought more than once: *What gives her the right?* The girl has become so sassy she seems ungrateful, unaware how kind they are to her; Eliza's mother thinks she should never be let out of the kitchen, certainly not into the dining room, to eat with everyone who has to *look at that horrible hand.*

What comes from the kitchen then is a silver tureen filled with clouds that Lucy carries gravely to the sideboard. "Oh!" cries Dr. Franklin, clapping his hands, "you've made *Île flottante!* Is it James Hemings' receipt?"

Lucy dips her head and lets herself smile a little. She and Mag stirred the yolks and cream over a slow fire for an hour, taking turns, never letting it stick. The *crème anglaise* is a sea of yellow silk; Lucy has beaten the egg whites into Himalayan peaks that shimmer as she brings them in. She learned from James Hemings at Monticello how to whip them with the back of a wooden spoon in a copper bowl. "See?" he'd said as the clear liquid, purged of any speck of yolk or shell, took in air and rose under his hand: just firm enough for the whites to rise, but not so hard as to beat them down.

"You have to be brave to cook well." James had glanced at her sidelong, but searchingly, as if to ask: *Will you carry this on?* and never mentioning that the overseer, even here, even after his years in Paris, counts every discarded egg and charges him for it. Cooking with this rigor is an art, Lucy has learned, and passes her knowledge on to Mag, who stands to watch the guests' pleasure as they serve themselves and taste and taste.

Charles Willson is beaming, as if he's made the dessert himself: he who spends no time in the kitchen. "Congratulations, Lucy!" he calls, and begins a round of applause. Lucy smiles with her whole face for the first time since she's come to this house, and turns to the girl behind her: "And thanks to Mag, who stirred the *creme anglaise,*" pronouncing the French as James had taught her.

When the last of the delicate confection has disappeared and the spoons have clicked against the empty dishes—Charles Willson having returned for a second helping, even though he'd warned all the children, *Family hold back* —and guests have pushed back their chairs, the tables are cleared of dishes and cloths. In the English way, cordial glasses, nuts, and bowls of berries appear on the bare wood; the women retire to the drawing room for coffee in Eliza's grandmother's gold-leaf thimble-sized cups, while Charles Willson pours brandy for the men, who crack jokes and walnuts, relieved of the need for decorum. The talk goes on long into the night: of barn-raising, of planting and livestock, of saddle-making and tin-smithing, and of pewter molds and, much later, of women, after the wives, sisters and daughters have gone home.

Work in the kitchen goes long into the night, too: scraping and washing dishes with water steadily boiling on the hearth, taking care not to be scalded; carrying the scraps and slops to the pigs; putting what food is left in the cold room and the pie safe. Peggy marshals all the children: the girls and Charlie and Moses take the first shift and are sent to bed; the young men haul the heavy buckets of compost to the gardens and finish what's left of the wine. Then Raphaelle and Rembrandt wash their hands under the pump and saunter to join the men drinking at the bare table.

Rubens takes *Old English Farming* from its shelf and reads a little in the kitchen corner, before beginning to nod and heading to bed.

All evening, Lucy has turned to look behind her, hoping to see Scarborough in a shadowed corner; he'd said he wouldn't sit in the same room as Jeff Randolph, but she hoped he would come out of the kitchen to see her moment of success.

"Moses," she whispers to her son, "go find your father." Moses has brought the dessert plates out with Mag, who dares carry only a few at a time, and now the two lock eyes and, without a word, run to the stable.

Scarborough is standing in the entrance with a length of thick rope in his hands; he starts when the children come through the dusk. "Papa," Moses grasps his shirtsleeve, "won't you come and eat?" Scarborough smiles wryly: "If I can stay in the kitchen," and allows his son to hold his hand all the way to the house, where the clean dishes rest on racks by the stove. Peggy flicks a clean towel over the cutting boards, and Lucy scrubs an iron pot with a stiff brush and boiling water from the kettle. She brushes back the hair that has slipped from her kerchief when Scarborough and the children came in, and stands straight to look at him, relief and fear competing in her face. Before she can speak, Peggy takes the plate she's kept warm from the side of the hearth. "You hungry?" she asks in her brisk, cheerful, almost joking way, as though nothing troubling has happened.

He folds his long legs under the big table and begins to eat, as Lucy bends to the pot one of them has let sit too long on the heat. When she's scraped the stubborn bits from the metal and hung the pot from its high hook, she brushes Scarborough's neck where the brand still shines. "Will you play for us while we finish up?" Peggy asks, and he takes his banjo from its corner.

The men in the dining room, the women gossiping in the drawing room, hear through the warm summer night the high plaint of a tune from Africa by way of Tobago, about ocean and shackles and backs breaking in the cane fields. Arabella Randolph gathers her small purse and shawl and murmurs her excuses, leading the other women to the door. Their men only laugh and tell them to go along home; Jeff Randolph calls in his cheeky way: "Old Charles Willson is good for another round," and someone brings out a deck of cards. Those who came in carriages will bid their drivers return the next day; those who came in carts or on horseback and have to work in the morning will play a hand and take their leave.

At breakfast, after *café au lait* and Lucy's feathery biscuits, there will be shots of brandy for the heavy heads. When Lucy brings out the tray of night-cap shot glasses, Jeff shouts: "Here's to you, girl! How's that man of yours? Giving you trouble, I'll bet, and giving my friend Charles Willson even more!" Lucy begins to shudder so the glasses rattle and slide, and Mag, just behind her, steadies the tray with the flat stump of her right hand until Lucy sets it down.

Jeff is staring with a curiosity—mocking, hostile—Mag hasn't seen for years now, but which has been imprinted on her skin. "Ho, what's this, Charles Willson, cripples for servants? Bet you can get her for a quarter of the price."

Mag flushes with shame and slips her offending hand under her apron skirt, but Charles Willson—who drank more than he intends to, wanting to keep up with his guests, and now feeling sore all over and angry with himself—puts down his glass and stands. "I'll thank you to leave my house, sir."

Jeff Randolph sneers: "So that's the way it is with you, Peale. Isn't she kind of young, though?" But he pushes back his chair as Charles Willson moves closer to him, and the other men rise to go. The evening is over in the morning.

Chapter 13

MAG AND MOSES NEVER TALK about what they may have interrupted in the stable, but they don't have to; they have many unspoken understandings. The boy, living with his parents, has heard his father's explosions of help-less rage as his mother becomes more accepted, even valuable, in this house—*taken over*, said with venom; *traitor* is a word hurled into the tiny room. Mag, down the hall, has found it hard to sleep, and one distracted morning has caused Peggy to glance at her with concern: "Not feeling well, dear?" as she lets the coffee boil to bitterness in the pot.

Mag shakes her head, mentions only how hot the attic gets. "Maybe we can find another room for you, down with the girls," Peggy thinks aloud. "The attic will be miserable soon." Mag sees an opening to ask something else: "What is the little house next to the cow barn used for?"

"Oh, that was the girls' playhouse, but they seem to be too grown up for that now."

One day after lessons and lunch, while the main house drowses—everyone reading or dozing—Mag and Moses slip out the kitchen door to the playhouse set in a grove of poplars behind the cow barn. Scarborough, cleaning tack, sees them run past, and wonders if he was ever as carefree, as innocent, as that.

Mag runs faster, her braids swinging across her back, shining red-brown in the sun. When Moses catches up, he flicks a braid in her face, meaning only to brush her lightly, and scratches her eye instead. Used to not screaming, she makes a startled, strangled sound and doubles over, bunching a corner of her apron and holding it against her eye. Moses is as startled as she; coming behind her, he takes her shoulders in his hands, and drops them almost immediately in embarrassment: "Are you all right? I didn't mean to hurt you . . ."

She shakes her head, not to say *no*, but to throw away the hurt. "Come on; we don't have much time before they'll miss us." Still holding her apron to her eye, she moves as fast as she can, stumbling a little, toward the little house. No one has walked the path for a while; a scent of crushed fern rises as they reach the stone threshold.

"Is it locked?" he asks. Every door at the Randolphs' was locked, often more than once.

"Haven't you noticed? Nothing's locked here," she answers, pressing the latch and pushing against the wooden door, which sticks a bit, then swings open on a room where light falls from all sides. There are a child-sized table and chairs to match, a cupboard with doll-sized cups and saucers, a fireplace filled with ashes. Mag turns to Moses, as she always turns when no one is watching, when her joy overcomes her with an electric charge that lights her face: "It's perfect!"

"For?" he smiles, a bit bewildered, not quite seeing what she sees in this bare place.

"Your family," she explains, pacing off the lengths from east to west, and north to south. "Some windowpanes need replacing," he remarks, running his fingers along the frames with the attention to detail that Charles Willson has already noticed. "They all need glazing."

"But yes!" Mag whirls in the center of the floor, her scratched eye forgotten. "You don't have to stay in that hot attic room. You can be together."

He notices that groundhogs have chewed the doorframe and bird feathers have fallen from the chimney, but he catches her excitement, catches her good hand as she whirls. Which startles her—it's not what she planned or knows what to do with, so she dances away, but her smile is a quick glint before she turns to inspect the hearth. Moses lets go of her hand—as lightly as he held it—in that brief, rare stage between innocence and awareness. The twists of his growing-in hair catch the light as he bends to the hearth with her. Something rustles there and tries to get free: knocking, scraping against the chimney stones.

Moses reaches up into the tarry opening; with a clatter of wings and flurry of ash, the sound of a rusty hinge being forced, the grackle bursts into the room, scattering ashes. Mag, without being told, runs to open the door and waves her arms at the dusty bird, which seizes its chance at light and air, and flies to freedom.

"They steal other birds' nests and foul them; chimneys must look like safe places, until they're trapped." Moses rests on his heels, brushing the ash and creosote off his hands. "You can't blame him for wanting to be free."

Mag, obscurely irritated by his knowledge of country things, snaps: "How do you know it's a he?"

He never anticipates her flashes of anger, and is stunned by the violence in her tone. "I don't," he answers mildly. "It flew away too fast to see."

She is even more annoyed by his refusal to get angry than by his command of so many details she hasn't noticed, and persists: "Why say *he* then?"

He shrugs, the larger person, and she defers: "We'll need to do a lot of cleaning, but this can be a nice place."

"If Charles Willson says Yes," he cautions, with a hint of superior knowledge he can't suppress, and strangely rights the balance of power between them.

Mag grabs a broom by the hearth and begins to sweep up the cinders: "At least we can make it look better before they see it." He finds the dustpan and bends beside her.

It's Mag who raises the subject, remembering the only time she'd found Charles Willson alone. She slips away to the library one day after lunch, before Peggy or Lucy can think of a task for her. Charles Willson is where he always is when he's home at this time of day: reading, then napping, with his glasses on his nose and a book or notebook face-down on his chest. He sleeps lightly and senses her presence; although she's tried not to startle him, she wants him to wake.

"Mag, looking for a book?" he asks without opening his eyes.

"No, sir, just cleaning one," she answers, holding a copy of Locke up to dust it.

"I might find one you'd like, if you like to read."

"I don't have much time, sir."

"You need to make time for that, Mag, for your mind. You might like poetry, where there aren't so many words." He tells her to look for Phillis Wheatley on the shelf of "W's," and bring him the book. Still a little dazed from sleep, he reads:

Imagination! who can sing thy force?
Or who describe the swiftness of thy course?

"She was a slave who became a famous poet."

"Did she ever get to be free?"

Charles Willson stirs uncomfortably and sits up; the book of Blake's poems slides from his stomach to the floor. He doesn't like unhappy stories, especially when he has to tell them to the young. "She did, but her life was hard."

"Did anyone help her?" Mag asks, retrieving *Songs of Innocence and of Experience* from the floor.

"I wasn't sure where she was, to help her." Charles Willson straightens his rumpled vest and slaps his knees with his palms, even more uncomfortable. He hates to be reminded of inaction, inattention.

Mag looks at him with an unspoken appeal: not a girl noticed in a crowd, except for her eyes, which are large, deep brown, and, at this moment, eloquent.

He can't excuse himself: "I wish I'd known and done something."

Mag holds the book to her chest, wrapping both arms around it as if to protect it and its contents. "I'll read this," she says, and then remembers why she was in the library, pretending to dust books, to begin with: "Sir, it's getting hot in the attic now. . . ."

"Oh, why don't you move into the spare room downstairs, next to Isba?" He briskly hopes to solve at least this problem.

"No, I don't mean for me, sir: for Lucy, Scar, and Moses. It's awful crowded in that room."

"Have they said anything?" looking at her sharply, thinking it's another thing he hasn't noticed.

"No, no," she hasn't meant that at all. "No, *I* think it must be hard for them to live there," her words coming in a rush: "We could fix up the girls' playhouse they don't play in anymore. Moses and I cleaned it a little today and it could be fine . . . Sir?" She stops, horrified by her own boldness; this is a house where all the ideas are his.

"Mag," he puts both long hands on her narrow shoulders. "You have a beautiful heart." Squeezes once, and lets her go.

When he adds up his good deeds, taking her into his family will be one, to set against Phillis Wheatley, to set against Lydia.

Why hadn't he helped when he knew Phillis' husband was in

jail? He was traveling in Maryland and Virginia, painting portraits, settling his own debts. . . And Lydia? She died when he
was in Newburyport, that desperate trip of a young man trying
to escape his creditors, *hiring*—no, buying—that young woman
from a friend, *a private sale* (wasn't that better than an auction?),
to help Rachel in her first pregnancy. He told himself he couldn't
have helped had he been there.

But when Lydia fell ill, and Rachel sent a message—urgent, by
packet-boat: *Should I call for the doctor?* He'd written back: *We can't
afford it*. Would a doctor, would anything, have made a difference?
Lydia was 20.

Chapter 14

AS IF IT'S HIS IDEA, the girls' playhouse becomes another of Charles Willson's projects; all the children in the household have to take part, whether they want to or not. The older boys grumble at the window-glazing, the whitewashing, the clapboard repair and painting: Rembrandt and Raphaelle consider themselves artists, too refined for menial work; Rubens works hard with his hands, but in the gardens, where he's the master of planting, cultivation, and harvest. The girls, though, cheerfully give up their claim to the house they haven't played in for years, and set to: sweeping, mopping, washing the windows, hemming flour sacks for curtains. Moses climbs on the roof with long chimney brushes; Charlie holds the ladder, but only after shaking it, and laughing when Moses yells in fear and anger. Charlie acts, his uncle says, "more like a Peale" the longer he lives in their house, but he isn't above tripping Moses when he's carrying a heavy roast, or pulling his chair out from under him.

Raphaelle teases: "We should send you down the chimney, except we wouldn't know if it's clean," meaning Moses, who shudders, remembering boys on the Randolphs' place covered in creosote and soot. Mag, washing a window, surprises herself by flinging back: "The bird we chased out got it cleaner than anyone could." Raphaelle starts to say, *Didn't know you were sweet on Moses,* but catches himself as his father comes up the path.

"This path will need sweeping, and more small stones for edging, boys," he says, clearly enjoying the sight of all the young doing his bidding: the vision of the family farm, with himself at its master, realized before him. Eliza complains that so much effort is being expended on what she calls *the slave cabin,* but Charles Willson listens to her less and less: her voice a buzz in his ear, a fly to be brushed off.

In a room over the only tavern in the city that will take them, Ira cleans his pistol carefully with the tail of his shirt, Jeb picks some morsels of food from his teeth with the blade of his knife. "How long do we have to stay here?" he whines, as he's done often in the past several days.

Ira shows his disdain by not looking in his direction and by pausing a full minute before answering: "When we've got them. Otherwise, we have to give the money back."

"But we don't have no leads," Jeb protests, and it's true that no one they've encountered has talked about a family of runaways, even with a wink and a promise of reward.

"We'll ride out to that Peale place tomorrow; there's something going on there." Ira continues his cleaning without looking up; it takes all his military discipline not to lose his temper with this lout he's had to take along. He prides himself on his lack of emotion, his ability to act within well-defined limits. He doesn't hate the runaways he hunts but sees hunting them as a way of upholding the law, even of keeping the peace. He wouldn't say, if called to account by some tribunal that will never come, *I was just doing my job,* as if his will and pride weren't involved.

The runaways he catches are actually relieved when they see he's part of the patrol; they know he won't allow gratuitous cruelty from his deputies: just enough brute force to gain control.

He's stopped his men from raping, castrating, lynching and other forms of torture, but he's aware he can't be everywhere.

In the morning they ride out early and see the many hands at work on the playhouse, painting clapboards and window-frames: mainly only white hands today, since Scarborough has gone to apprentice at a saddle-maker's in the city, and Moses is in Charles Willson's painting room stretching canvases and cleaning brushes. Lucy is of course in the kitchen, so what appears to the riders is a Peale family project: renovating a playhouse for another use.

Ira glances at the young men and the girls busy in their painting smocks, pausing only to notice how the one with the missing hand wields her brush; remembering that she opened the door to them when they came; his mind is like a cabinet where he's filed her startled look. "We'll come back tonight," he says over his shoulder to Jeb, turning his horse back onto the highway. Jeb starts to ask, "Why not question them?" but finds his words landing in the flick of Ira's horse's tail.

No one has noticed their passage except Mag, who always senses a face turned towards her in a curious or hostile stare. When Charles Willson comes back from the city, she notices his frown and the slump of his shoulders—it must have been a trying portrait—but runs to him anyway.

"Sir, sir!" She is close to tugging on his coat-tail in her anxiety, and barely restrains herself from shouting. Charles Willson glances down at her, then turns to lift the saddle-bag of paints and brushes off the patient horse, as if he hasn't heard. He's had a long day of trying to make civil conversation with a sugar merchant worried about his investment in the Indies.

Mag persists: "Sir, those men rode by today as we were painting the playhouse."

This time Charles Willson catches the urgency in her voice, and knows exactly who she means by "those men." He pauses before unfastening the girth, not wanting to seem alarmed or unsure. Then, "Thank you, Mag. I don't think Lucy and Scarborough should move in or show themselves outside for a few days." He guesses that the patrol will be back soon, but also that they won't stay around if they don't find what they're looking for.

"Chicken and biscuits!" Lucy announces as he enters the kitchen, with an enthusiasm that overcomes her concentration and surprises herself as much as those around her. He makes himself smile in appreciation, understanding how rare this joy is in her, how much it has had to overcome. He nods to Peggy and signals to her as Lucy bends to roll the dough: "A word?"

As Peggy wipes chicken fat on her apron, they make a plan. He and she will find ways to keep Scarborough, Lucy, and Moses busy indoors; they won't sleep in the playhouse for the next few nights, even though it's ready for them to move in.

"Mag knows, but the others don't need to be alarmed." Peggy nods; *Especially not Eliza* is unspoken and understood between them.

Lamplight cuts a small square on the playhouse dooryard that night when two horses pull up on the road past the farm. Ira raises his hand in a gesture he intends to silence Jeb's triumphant: "Got 'em now!" Ira dismounts and gestures again, this time to show that Jeb should follow him. They tie reins to the split-rail, and approach the playhouse door.

"Open up!" Ira's deep voice reinforces his knock. A chair scrapes inside—Jeb hops from one foot to the other in anticipation—and a large shape fills the doorway, blocking the light. "Looking for someone, gentlemen?"

Ira steps forward as if to seize the man's arm, then sees that the arm is as white as the rolled shirt-sleeve. "Beg your pardon, sir.

We have a warrant for a family of escaped slaves and have reason to believe they might have come this way."

Charles Willson's anger is stronger than his fear of confrontation. "There's no one escaped here, and what do you mean by a 'warrant'? If you mean a 'commission,' we don't accept those in Pennsylvania." Both men speak with the authority of belief; neither is supported by facts, which fluctuate from state to state and from person to person.

Ira had heard of Charles Willson, and remembers seeing him in the tavern. He touches his forefinger to the brim of his hat in a show of respect. "Sorry to disturb you, sir." With a whirl of horses and a lash of reins, their departure is louder, faster than their arrival. Ira spurs his horse, though there's no need to hurry back to their lodgings over the tavern, where they order round after round of ale, Ira refusing to speak to or look at Jeb, Jeb throwing questions at the wall of Ira's face: "What do we do now?" "Where did those fucks go?" "Who is that bastard you tipped your hat to?" "We don't get no bonus unless we get them, right? Right?"

When the bar-keep finally cuts them off, and they face each other in the small bedroom, Ira answers, "That high-and-mighty son-of-a-bitch is hiding something. We'll go back, but it'll have to be soon; we've spent almost all the advance. You'll have to cut back on the drink. And shut your mouth now, before I shut it for you."

Chapter 15

I f CHARLES WILLSON HAS A DANGEROUS FLAW, it's self-congratulation; he tells Scarborough his strategy has worked: "That patrol won't be back. You and your family can stay there tonight." Scarborough, cleaning tack, merely nods. Although Charles Willson presents himself as enlightened, and encourages Scarborough to speak his mind, a distrust of whites this deeply ingrained can't be easily abandoned.

In any event, preparations for Charles Willson's birthday are taking the whole household's attention this summer day, when the celebration has been postponed from April 14th, the actual date, because Eliza was in the earliest, most nauseous phase of her pregnancy.

Rubens complains that this is the worst, because the busiest time in the growing season. Rembrandt and Raphaelle grumble, but would resist, no matter the date; they'd rather be fishing or swimming or riding to dances at neighboring farms. Titian pays more attention to the turtles he's captured and is studying, but isn't expected to do more than set out chairs for the musicians. Angelica and Isba are always willing to do what needs to be done. Charlie, chastened, doesn't think he could complain; Mag is too grateful to imagine protesting.

Peggy and Lucy—Peggy always asks Lucy's opinion now—are pleased to plan a menu that includes ripe tomatoes and raspberries.

Although Charles Willson will turn 65, this year's party will be small, in deference, again, to Eliza, whose pregnancy has only a few more months to go. Just twenty friends are invited—Dr. Franklin is expected but Mr. Jefferson is not—to have dinner and listen to music. Besides helping in the kitchen, the children must practice: Angelica on harpsichord, Rembrandt and Raphaelle on flute and violin, Rubens on viola. Charles Willson is conductor and first violin, even though his playing is rough from lack of attention. Isba sings a confident but imprecise soprano; Charlie and Moses make up a chorus.

The dinner—of roast chickens, tomatoes and eggplant, watercress salad—has been put on the sideboard as usual; the guests will serve themselves. Peggy, Lucy, Mag, and Moses sit at the table after bringing the dishes in. Scarborough, who has made clear his reluctance to have anything to do with serving food, has eaten from the plate Lucy has set out for him and taken more of his family's possessions to the little house.

With Mozart rising in the drawing room and the dishwater filling the kitchen sink, no one hears the pistol shot, except Argus and Apollo, who begin to bark in alarm and terror. Mag slips from her place at the sink and runs to the porch to quiet them, with a roll handy in her pocket.

In the open playhouse door, three large shapes block the light: the tallest clearly Scarborough, except that he slumps to the ground as she registers who he is and what she's seeing. Two horses that she hasn't noticed are tied to the fence shake their bridles and whinny. Scarborough lets out half a groan, the sound of someone trying hard not to show pain, and one man pulls back his leg for a kick. Mag screams and runs toward them; this sound reaches Moses, who steps out of his place and tugs Charles Willson's sleeve.

"What do you think you're doing on my property?" Charles Willson shouts from the porch, then turns to Moses: "Get your mother, get Peggy. . ." But Moses is already running.

Charles Willson confronts the patrol unarmed; he's said he had enough of guns in the War, and refuses to own one, even though Rubens asks, "How do you expect me to keep down the woodchucks?"

Ira and Jeb turn their pistols in his direction as he repeats: "What do you think you're doing on my property?"

"This is an escaped slave we're taking in. Where're the woman and the boy?" Ira refuses to say "sir" now, but stops short of calling Charles Willson a liar.

"This is my man," Charles Willson begins, struggling not to say "my property" or "my slave" directly. "I have the papers," he says, hoping he can find the scrawled receipt.

"Well, find them," Ira orders, keeping his pistol level, aimed at Charles Willson's chest.

"First, this man's wound needs to be treated," Charles Willson says firmly, as if fully in charge of the situation, although he's wondering as he speaks where that paper he disdained and tossed aside might be. For all his respect for law, he's as careless with legal documents as he is meticulous with his paints.

A dark red stain has spread from Scarborough's forearm onto the ground, moving closer to the white men's boot-toes, and he raises his arm over his head, to give the blood a harder route from his heart. His shirt is speckled, then soaked, with dark blotches. Lucy runs up, through the dangerous circle of white men, with Peggy close behind her. Mag, further back, balances a pan of water unsteadily with her uneven hands. With desperate speed, Peggy found the strips of sheeting saved for just such a purpose, and binds one tight around his arm. Lucy embraces his shuddering shoulders and beckons to Mag to bring the water.

"We need to get him inside," Peggy sounds as if she knows

what will happen next, although she has no idea. Mag, without being told, runs for Rembrandt and Rubens, who can be relied on not to have drunk too much, and are strong enough to carry Scarborough.

"The papers," Ira repeats: an order, not a question or a request.

Charles Willson snaps his fingers in Moses' direction in a convincing display of certainty: "Get my case." Moses, who pays attention to everything Charles Willson does, knows which case he means: the one where he put the notes he copied at the meeting with the lawyer. The men around his father stand in a ring, facing each other, while the women kneel on the ground, tending to the wound.

When Charles Willson sees his leather case in Moses' arms, he feels the shame of the constitutionally unorganized. *What will I do if that paper isn't inside?* But Moses kneels and unties the lashing that binds the case. With a sure hand he pulls out a parchment scroll that Charles Willson had tossed there. "Here, sir."

He caught a glimpse of his name along with his parents' when Charles Willson visited the lawyer, and then in a moment alone, he unrolled the page that transfers them—*A man and wife, young and able-bodied, and a boy, given to Charles Willson Peale in payment for a portrait of me and my wife.*

Charles Willson's hand shakes as he takes the scroll, so he takes and unrolls it quickly and thrusts it at Ira. "Will this satisfy you?"

Ira holds it up to the light coming from the playhouse door and thrusts it back.

"Let's go," he gestures with his pistol to Jeb, who gives Scar one sharp kick before he follows Ira to the horses. Scarborough by this time, however, is too close to unconsciousness to register the kick as pain, although he groans as Rembrandt and Rubens make ready to lift him.

"Gently: one under his shoulders, one under his hips." Charles

Willson has carried wounded soldiers from the battlefield, and regains his authority. "Spare his arm."

Rembrandt can't help grumbling that Scarborough's blood will get on his best clothes; he doesn't have to look at his father to feel his disappointment. He has reached the age of chafing under the family order, not because he disagrees with its ideals, but because he wants to make his own choices. *He talks about freedom* he argues with his father in his head. Rubens, who has the gardens under his own control, simply does what he's told in areas that aren't important to him, as now, when he quietly bends to the task of lifting Scarborough without hurting him further. As it is, Scarborough lets out an anguished groan, shaking his bearers, who reposition their arms under him: Rembrandt at his head, Rubens at his hips.

"Where's your brother?" Charles Willson's question is rhetorical; he's seen how Raphaelle poured more wine into his glass and played his violin with exaggerated flourishes. He stands now in the kitchen door, swaying a little, just as his brothers come toward him with their awkward burden. Scarborough groans again, and Rembrandt snaps to Raphaelle, "Get the fuck out of the way," not caring that their father forbids such language: *The default speech of those who can't find the right words.*

Peggy, Lucy, and Mag have cleared the kitchen table as best they can; in the desperation of the moment, Scarborough is laid on the scrubbed planks. Peggy whispers to Charles Willson, "We'll need the surgeon for this," but Rubens has already headed for the stable.

"We'll get them yet, we'll get that stuck-up bastard who thinks he's so high and mighty; I'll get that Black bitch. . ." Jeb chatters, until Ira pulls up so close to him that their stirrups touch, and draws back his arm. "You won't do anything I don't tell you to, you dumb fuck," he snarls. It's a silent ride back to the city, only the horses are content to be going slow, back to whatever feed they'll be given.

Under the oil lamp Peggy holds, as high as she can, the surgeon's scalpel flashes as he probes the flesh for the bullet. Charles Willson holds Scarborough's shoulders from behind, trusting himself to be steady enough only after he's urged on the patient a shot of his strongest brandy and taken some himself. When he held out the shot glass, Scarborough looked at him through the fog of pain with disbelief: *What white man would give a slave alcohol? Only a crazy one, or else the pain deceives me.* . . . Charles Willson reads his expression, and holds the glass of glowing liquid a little closer to his face. It's Lucy, in her vigilance, who takes the glass without a word and holds it to her husband's lips. The brandy can't suppress a moan that rises from a deep shudder inside him; Charles Willson tightens his grip on shoulders almost too big for his hands.

Charles Willson's good shirt is spattered with blood by the time the surgeon has scooped the bullet from the torn flesh and sewn up the wound. At some point during the operation, Charles Willson feels Scarborough's shoulders slip from his hands. "Thank God," someone in the circle exclaims as a breath released: Peggy maybe, although it could have been any one of them. They all, even the surgeon, have the same thought.

He leaves behind laudanum and instructions for changing the dressings, speaking only to Peggy, who turns to include Lucy as he speaks. "Yes," she says. "Lucy and I will take good care of him."

In the kitchen, Charles Willson pours more brandy for the doctor and pulls his wallet from his waistcoat. "Your bill?"

The surgeon looks uncomfortable; he likes to pretend his services are humanitarian acts, devoid of financial considerations: "I had to leave my dinner and ride five miles to get here; that lead was lodged deep in the flesh. I'll have to charge you the usual."

Charles Willson pulls three large bills from his wallet. "Is this enough?"

The surgeon pockets the payment quickly, as if to get it out of sight and mind. "He must be a very good worker; most owners would just let a slave bleed."

Charles Willson throws down his brandy in a single gulp. "If you'll excuse me, I'll see to my guests," and holds the door until the surgeon walks through it.

The last notes of the Mozart sonata Angelica has been playing falter in the unsettled air. No one in the drawing room has been unaware of the disturbance outside, although performers and audience have continued the evening's entertainment as if Rembrandt and Rubens haven't been pulled from their midst. Angelica, especially, has the gift of concentration, accompanying Isba on the Handel aria she hasn't practiced enough and moving without pause into the Mozart, although the room's attention is turned half to the music's bright order, half to the abrupt hints of violence outside the circle of candlelight.

Raphaelle meets his father at the drawing room door, his throat bare, shirt unbuttoned to his breastbone, a full glass of bright liquor in his hand. He starts to smile, and is stalled by his father's expression.

"Raph," Charles Willson begins, and struggles to restrain his anger; he wants to grab his son by his shirt collar and shake him, beautiful as he is, more fallen angel than boy on the verge of manhood. "See what help they need in the kitchen," he uses as few words as possible, in a voice so low only Raph can hear, not to betray trouble in this house that goes beyond the Slave Patrol's visit and Scarborough's wound.

Eliza rushes from her seat on the sofa, unbalanced by the weight she bears before her, and clings to her husband: "What happened? Are you all right?"

He feels the child in her as she presses against him, and tries to be gentle, "It's all taken care of, all right now." He smooths her forehead as Dr. Franklin approaches with an outstretched hand: "Good night, my friend, I trust all is well." Without explanation, Charles Willson nods and joins the hand-clasps offered him as the men shepherd their ladies to the hall.

Only at this point does he realize that with Scarborough lying wounded, no one knows how to bring the horses and carriages to the dooryard. "Rubens!" he shouts in the direction of the kitchen, and in an undertone: "Raph, the horses!" It's Isba who instantly understands, and leads her brothers to the stable, where the horses doze in their grain bags and must be put in their traces. The horses shake their heads at Raph's alcoholic unsteadiness, his high-volume directions: "All right, let's get moving!" Isba simply stares at him without giving him the respect of a reply. Rubens moves into place beside her and reaches a sure hand to the first bridle; he doesn't spend time in the stables, but his connection with animals is intuitive and assured.

The carriages come to the front door slowly, Mr. Franklin's first, with Rubens driving; then Isba in the second, sitting straight and determined on the driver's bench, and in the third, an unchastened Raph, who flicks the whip with an unnecessary flourish and pulls the trap around in an exaggerated swoop, impressing his young cousins Margaretta, Anna, and Sarah, who laugh and clap as he draws up.

Chapter 16

TITIAN HASN'T COME TO THE PARTY, but he's always so quiet, so attentive to some small creature he's found on his journeys and brought home in his waistcoat pocket that no one has noticed his absence until the chairs are cleared away from the drawing room concert. Angelica turns to ask her sister and Mag if they've seen him, but Isba has gone to the stable and Mag is in the kitchen helping Peggy and Lucy tend to Scarborough. She's known Titian to fall asleep in a corner of the hall, with his jacket drawn up around his ears and his sketchpad and pencil fallen from his hand, but the corners and the childhood hide-out under the stairs are empty.

He is buried in a mound of quilts and blankets, although his room is stifling hot. There is a terrible smell from the chamber pot by the bed; some of its blood-streaked contents have overflowed its rim and spread on the floor. Angelica's first impulse is to fling open the windows to the warm night, then she gathers her skirts and steps carefully to the bed. Her hand on Titian's shoulder shakes from his trembling. "Ti?" she hazards, but he merely groans.

She finds her father waving goodbye to the last guest. "Is the doctor still here? It's Titian." She's close to tears, having seen this kind of illness before and knowing its gravity.

Charles Willson takes the stairs two at a time; the face he turns to his daughter is a mask of fear. "Send someone," he tells her, but she has already started for the stable, where she finds her brothers laughing—Raph the loudest—in the relief of a crisis past. Rubens is always the one most likely to listen: "Can you get the doctor back?"

"Is it Scarborough?"

"No, Titian," and as she names the trouble, it becomes real; the tears she's been holding back begin to flow.

Rubens takes the fastest horse and reaches the doctor's door just as he's stepping from his trap. He brings quinine for the fever, but shakes his head when he takes his hand from Titian's burning forehead. "Just keep giving him water and pray the fever breaks."

Charles Willson puts burdock root on the boy's icy feet to draw out the sickness, but Titian cries out and continues to shudder. From his chair next to the bed, Charles Willson waves Eliza away when she puts her head around the door: "Charles, I can't sleep," she starts to plead, and is cut off by another dismissive wave.

"My son is dying, can't you see?" he snarls, regretting his tone almost as the words leave his mouth. But she's already retreated, and the boy in his coverlets begins to gasp for breath, his flushed face paling as he stops shivering. As he stills, Charles Willson lowers his darker head to the boy's fair one; alone in the room, he allows himself to cry out to the God who has taken away another being he's loved.

This boy so full of love for the world and all its creatures.

He falls asleep in the chair, his head still on Titian's. Angelica, who has been listening outside the door, who hasn't slept, tiptoes in and opens the windows to the dawn light that touches the tree tops on the far hill before it reaches the valley, the farm buildings, this house.

Her father stirs and reaches his hand to her; she will be, for the rest of their lives, his confidante. "It must have been water from the pond where he was watching frogs." He rubs his stiff neck and reaches for reason. Angelica supports him as he finds an uncertain balance. "Peggy and Lucy will need to wash and dress him. The boys. . ." He can't finish outlining the burial ritual and sinks to his knees.

Rubens, in Scarborough's absence and his father's immobility, measures his brother's body and finds boards for the coffin. He's not a skilled carpenter, but he knows how to build a simple box. There's no time for mortised corners; no one but the worms will see the nails driven into the wood, some aslant where Rubens has hit them uncertainly. He has loved this younger brother: so quiet and watchful, at home outdoors with wild things as he is, sometimes sketching the vegetables he's most proud of. The other brothers, older and more worldly, have paid him little attention but must help dig his grave in the plot above the barn.

Charles Willson will quickly come to himself, and then be everywhere, issuing orders for the digging, the funeral lunch, the flowers and music. When he comes to the kitchen with his terrible news, Peggy, who rarely shows an emotion that breaks her composure, covers her face with her apron. Lucy steps forward: "We can have cold chicken, deviled eggs, asparagus, a lettuce salad, fresh berries by noon, sir."

"It will be just us, the family; there's no time to invite anyone else." Charles Willson grips Lucy's shoulder to steady himself, but she doesn't flinch or mistake his intent. "Thank you," he says simply, and takes Peggy in his arms; she slumps against him, and in that moment, it's hard to tell which one of them is sobbing, or if it's both.

Scarborough, in a soft chair by the stove, his wounded arm

sunk in a feather pillow, leans forward. "I'm able to help, sir. Just ask." Charles Willson raises his head from Peggy's shoulder: Peggy, who has been such a faithful member of this household, who raised Titian when Rachel died, says: "You just need to heal, Scarborough; there will be other times to help."

The morning air has warmed and thickened, with thunder rumbling faintly over the hills, by the time Titian's body has been laid in its wooden box and his brothers have brought it to the drawing room. Angelica and Isba have filled every container they could find with flowers: tulips, mostly, at this time of year, and roses, some bouquets of field clover, daisies and vetch. They wear their best dresses, even though both bear some evidence of Charles Willson's birthday dinner the night before.

The day is so warm that the boys wear just their white shirts and knee britches, but their father is dressed in his formal best: waistcoat, jacket, the silk britches with ribbon ties. He hasn't called a minister to do the service, but has decided to conduct the ceremony himself, according to his belief in a rational, reasonable God—although there seems to be only un-reason in the loss of this boy. There's been time to invite only his brother James and his family, no friends or neighbors, but the room is full.

Entering the humid space, Eliza falters, overcome by heat and scents, and is helped to a chair by one of the boys. Nervous, sweat clouding his glasses, Charles Willson clears his throat: "Dearly beloved. . ." He tries to project some authority, knowing the funerals of his childhood didn't begin this way, but unable to say anything else. These *are* his dearly beloved.

"One of our most beloved has been taken from us. . ." One of the girls begins to choke with sobs, and he falters, reaching in his memory for words he doesn't believe, but which are so deeply ingrained they come out of his mouth anyway:

"I am the resurrection and the life, saith the Lord. He that

believeth in me, though he were dead, yet shall he live, and who-
soever liveth and believeth in me shall never die." Charles Willson
feels James' sharp glance, and reaches for another passage from
the Book of Common Prayer, this one close to what he wants to
say: "We brought nothing into the world, and it is certain we can
carry nothing out. The Lord gave, and the Lord hath taken away."
He's aware that he's leaving out the last sentence of the funeral
reading: "Blessed be the name of the Lord." He'll have to struggle
to find this loss—this *theft*, as he thinks of it—as the act of a God
he would bless.

He looks down at the still face that was so alive with joy
only days ago, and speaks to it: "You were the love of my heart
and your mother's. Your love of every living thing"—the sound
of weeping comes from all sides of the room—"made us see all
Creation with new eyes, from the brightest sunset to the tiniest
mouse. You drew its delicate ears. . ." but he can't continue, and
buries his nose in his handkerchief as if it merely needed a good
blowing to clear his head; he could never admit to weeping in
front of his children. He waves vaguely at Angelica, who knows
to take her place at the harpsichord; Rembrandt, Raphaelle, and
Rubens take up their instruments. Bach will accompany them all
into the dooryard, where wind has begun to drive the looming
storm into the valley.

Angelica plays on as Charles Willson directs his brother and his
sons to lift the coffin and bear it to the burial ground on the hill
above the house. The young men have dug a hole in the red dirt
near an oak; they set the box in it so unevenly that Titian's body
slides forward with an unnerving knock. "Must be his new shoes,"
Raph says, to lighten the mood or reassure; not even he is sure
which. His father, assuming the first, and the worst of him, grabs
the shovel in angry haste; Rembrandt takes it from him gently,
and scrapes the dirt back in the hole, as the others throw in stones

that fit their hands. Charles Willson stands back against the oak, as the thunder rumbles again and the rain comes on, mixing with the tears on almost every face as the group hurries to the house.

Alone in his library with a full globe of apple brandy beside him—alcohol does no harm, he tells himself, within reason—he reaches for the volume of Marcus Aurelius, the worn leather a comfort to his hand. He finds what he needs:

Contentment with everything that happens—that is enough and *Whatever anyone says, I must be good.* Has he been as good as he means to be? Has he shown his family how to grieve and not be lost to grief? Has he cared for everyone enough, has he made up for Lydia? He drinks deeply, and is startled by a thumping in the hall, a sound of stumbling, of canes and umbrellas clattering from their jar to the floor, and the jar itself clattering.

Then a body falls against the door, which creaks but stays shut. He runs to pull it open, and finds Raph struggling to straighten up and losing his balance again.

"Fa. . ." he begins, his mouth unable to shape the word, but his father reaches for the brandy and throws it, stinging, in his face. "You bloody sot," Charles Willson's voice is low and full of venom, as Raph tries to wipe his eyes with his sleeve, and the library door closes against him. *Check desire; extinguish appetite. . .*

Charles Willson vows never to take another drop of alcohol, and Raphaelle, although he tries, and lies to his father and to himself, can never stop.

Chapter 17

IN THIS TIME OF MOURNING, Charles Willson imagines Titian in every corner and breaks off conversations in mid-sentence; the girls feed Titian's collection of mice, turtles, and birds with mending wings; Raphaelle stays out of his father's sight, riding into the countryside; Rembrandt paints until midnight, trying to perfect his skill at capturing likenesses; Rubens milks the cows and seldom lifts his eyes from plowing and planting; and even Peggy, overcome with memories of Titian, lets the bread burn and the soup boil over. Lucy stands behind her, salvaging what she can of the ruined meals, steadily inventing dishes that will nourish and distract. Mag and Moses are quick to see what needs to be done, and do it: bringing in the wood, washing the vegetables Rubens picks, churning the cream into butter, sweeping, mopping, gathering the eggs, taking meals to Grandmother Margaret and to Eliza, who keeps to her room and waves away most of the dishes Mag brings her.

The household routine with its balm goes on as usual, except that instead of looking to Charles Willson for guidance and direction, everyone turns to Scarborough—quiet, steady—as he nurses his wounded arm in his place by the stove.

Sunlight, even graylight, fills the kitchen from dawn to dusk;

the house is well sited to catch it. When he's alone, Scarborough watches the way a glass looks like the water that's made it; he's always been worked too hard to go to midnight school on the plantations he was bound to, and has picked up only a few words of written English. Charles Willson's latest *Philadelphia Enquirer* lies folded on the table; Mag isn't taking it in with his breakfast these days, after seeing it on his tray untouched. One day she notices it folded a different way, and closer to Scarborough's chair; another day she finds it in his lap: "Trying to figure this out," he says with a rueful grin and a shrug. "Reading is hard," she agrees, but doesn't presume he'd want her to help him.

Something in his stillness as he sits healing there, and his calm welcome of any passing attention makes members of the household stop, not only to cheer him, but in Charles Willson's absence, to ask his advice. It's almost as if, Peggy thinks, with the even light falling on him, he's been given a kind of holiness, like a priest waiting to receive confession, but kinder than any priest she ever talked to through a wooden grate. A priest who asked about *impure thoughts, Margaret,* and suggested what those thoughts might be. To Scarborough she can say, rubbing her sore feet, "I'm not sure I can do all this. My Aunt Margaret needs more help every day."

"Why don't you ask Angelica and Isba to help Lucy and Mag more in the kitchen?" he offers. "And Moses would be glad to push Mrs. Peale's chair."

Peggy pauses. As if the others have already taken up parts of her burden, she pours herself a cup of the tea that always steeps on the back burner and lightens it with a fresh jolt of milk. "Why don't you sit a minute?" Scarborough asks. "Everything doesn't have to be ready exactly on time." The tension that's her constant goad lifts from her body a little; they sit in silence—Irish woman with her work-reddened hands, Black man with a blood-stained bandage on his arm. Looking over at him, she rouses herself from the moment's rest. "We should take a look at that." "Not just yet," he answers.

Through the day, as they come through the kitchen, everyone in the household moves from pleasantries to questions; Scarborough's stillness and his deep-set eyes seem to offer answers. They find him always willing to talk; his suggestions, especially in Charles Willson's unsteady state, are reliable in their common sense.

What should he do with the cow whose milk turns sour as it hits the pail? Rubens can't remember. "You could ask Yarrow; he'll have a remedy," Scarborough suggests.

How can they get Eliza to eat? Peggy and Lucy are trying their best custards and broths, but nothing tempts her. "Some dandelion root tea with honey helped my mam," Scarborough says. Peggy doesn't stop to question him; she sends Moses out with the small curved knife she uses for gathering the greens.

But it's not only his practical advice that steadies them. Isba comes crying that her sister has invited Mag, not her, to gather watercress: "Mag can't even pick it very well."

"She'll do her best," Scarborough says in his mild but certain way. "Why don't you stay here and help Lucy with the shortcakes for dessert?"

Mag herself will tell him what she won't admit to anyone: "When Isba looks at me like I can't do something, I can't do it, even if I always have when she's not looking." "Don't mind her, honey," Scarborough soothes, but sensing this soothing isn't enough, he goes on: "I think how you do things when I'm trying to spare my arm."

"Oh, thank you, Scarborough!" Mag cries, and seems about to hug him, but hesitates to hurt his wound. It's when she pronounces his name that he offers what will become everyone's practice:

"Why not just call me *Scar*? I'll have another big one when this heals. My whole name reminds me of a place I'd rather forget anyway."

Charles Willson himself may need dandelion root tea. Deep in a lethargy almost as heavy as the one he felt when Rachel died, he hardly eats or sleeps or reads or moves. He doesn't leave the library sofa, let alone the house. When he steps uncertainly into the kitchen in search of coffee, shakes his head as if hoping to clear it of confusion, searches his memory for Scarborough's name, he sees—with both relief and apprehension—that the other man has somehow grown larger. The balance of power he's maintained so surely has shifted, as is never clearer than when Raphaelle comes into the kitchen without seeing Scarborough in the corner.

Raph hasn't forgotten the cooking wine Peggy and Lucy keep uncorked in the cupboard, and reaches for it. Before he can raise it to his lips, Scar clears his throat: "Sure you want to do that?" his voice is slow, with a certain lightness; the question seems disinterested, not accusatory.

"Who are you to stop me?" Raph understands the question perfectly. "I could have you sold away any time I want—except no one would buy you with a bum arm." He takes a long drink, and wipes his mouth on his sleeve. "Is there nothing better to drink around here? Since my father said he's giving up alcohol, there's just this rot-gut the women put in the food. . . ." He rummages in the cupboard, knocking jam jars and mustards, crocks of vinegar and kraut aside; a pitcher of ale falls to the counter.

Copper-colored foam spreads to the floor Mag has just scoured. Before Raph realizes that Scar has moved from his seat, Scar is beside him, good left hand on his arm. "Boy, you need to stop this."

Raph flushes red. "Who are you to call me *Boy*? That's what I'd call *you*, and worse, if my father didn't forbid it." He wrenches his arm from Scar's grasp, and as he does, drives his elbow into

Scar's wound, causing him to groan and stagger back against the stove. Raph stares at the blood now mixing with the beer, tosses the bottle to the floor, as if dismissing the whole mess, the whole episode, and runs outside with no object in mind but getting far away.

Lucy, hearing the groan, runs from the kitchen garden to find her husband curled on the floor, the weeks of healing forfeited and needing to be begun again.

Peggy helps her unwrap the soaked bandage and inspect the wound, which is seeping but clean. "Can we get the doctor back?" Lucy asks, but before she can answer, Charles Willson pushes the women gently aside and moves his glasses from his forehead to his nose. "I think just a soft cleaning and some calendula salve will do it. Do we have any in the house?"

Peggy, who is embarrassed to admit any lack of supplies, shakes her head. "Send Moses to Yarrow, who surely does," he says. "But if not, you can make some; we have beeswax and calendula flowers." Lucy nods; Mag is already at her elbow with a sponge and soapy water. Lucy's touch is as light as breath, but even breath would cause pain; Scar groans and apologizes for groaning. Mag brings a cloth dipped in cool water for his forehead. Moses had left for the next farm as soon as he heard Yarrow's name.

Chapter 18

CHARLES WILLSON SLOWLY COMES BACK to himself: making drawings for the windmill he hopes will speed the threshing, walking out into the fields and gardens, praising Rubens for the vegetables, but deciding to hire a farm manager for the larger crops, buying a wine press for the currants abundant now. His sense of possibility, if not of mastery, gives him his usual vigor, but Scar, as he heals, becomes the unacknowl-edged second-in-command. At his kitchen post, he listens, and even the older boys—the almost-men—confess their sins and confide the grievances they would never tell Charles Willson.

Mag brings her writing notebook in the quiet hours after lunch and sits at one end of the long work table. Usually, she doesn't like to be watched working or writing, but Scar in his benign silence seems to give her permission. Her pen fills a page with lines; she looks at the sky and then at him.

"Practicing your letters?" he asks.

"No, trying to make a poem. Like this—I mean I want to make one as good:"

Should you, my lord, while you peruse my song
Wonder from whence my love of Freedom sprung,

Whence flow these wishes for the common good,
By feeling hearts alone best understood,
I, young in life, by seeming cruel fate
Was snatched from Afric's fancy'd happy seat.
Such, such my case. And can I then but pray
Others may never feel tyrannic sway?

"You didn't write that; you learned it?"

"It's by Phillis Wheatley. She was a slave, but got free. Charles Willson lent her book to me."

"I'd like to read it, but I've never learned how." And so Mag begins to teach Scar to read, in the quiet times between meals when the kitchen is empty. When Lucy sees them bent over the page, she smiles and, by saying nothing, gives them her blessing. When Charles Willson has no errand for him, Moses joins them, tempted to tease his father for mispronouncing *tough* and *rough*, but at a nudge from Mag's slippered foot under the table, stifles his laughter. So they work on through the summer, as the bandages on Scar's arm have to be changed less often, as they come off clean, and Peggy pronounces the wound: "A scar for Scar."

"Another one," he corrects, fingers on the brand on the back of his neck.

Raph has stormed out of the house and down the highway towards Germantown, without realizing how far he's gone until the clinks of a team and the smell of turned earth brings him up short. Jem, the Randolphs' head man, walks behind the team, flicking flies from the horses' backs with his whip. He nods to Raph as the team makes the turn. Abner, who's just a boy, keeps his head down as he casts seed from a bag slung from his shoulder into a furrow. They're planting cotton pretty late in the season, Raph thinks, attuned to his father's thinking, even as he rebels against that rational, ever reasonable man. He's often argued that with a few slaves, the family wouldn't have to hire extra help or work all his children so hard: an argument that provokes a furious defense of abolition from his father.

"But didn't you have a girl, Lydia, when I was born?"

"You were too young to remember that," his father will say, hoping that Raph won't say, *And she died?* And remembering himself as a man his son's age, eager to rise in the world, writing to a friend: "I want to buy a boy to wait on me." *Could he actually have thought that, written that?* At this point in the confrontation, Charles Willson will hesitate and try to shift the ground, but Raph is always too quick for him:

"Why didn't you just tell Jeff Randolph you wouldn't accept Scarborough, Lucy and Moses as payment for their portrait?"

Charles Willson, as he will one day write to Angelica, struggles to *keep a bridle tight-reined on [his] tongue;* his voice comes as a hiss: "Would you have them separated and sold at auction?"

Which always causes Raph to throw whatever he's holding, once a glass that narrowly misses his father's head, and run outside. This day, he shakes his head, as if that would clear it, and turns back into the farm lane. He'll sleep most of the warm afternoon under a tree, barely waking when Moses snatches the straw hat shielding his eyes.

Moses and Mag, Mag and Moses: whenever they're free of a chore, they find ways to play; sometimes he leads, sometimes she does, climbing the apple trees in the kitchen garden, lapping cream from the top of the pails in the milk house, catching two doves in the dovecote with grain and trying to train them. "We could send messages to each other that no one else could see," Mag, who's read of such things, proposes, and this becomes a project that over time occupies their most dedicated attention.

Sometimes as they stand side by side, watching the doves fly out and circle back to them, Moses' arm brushes the side of Mag's breast by accident, but, absorbed in the birds, neither in these last months of their innocence takes note of it, until a day in early fall—the heat heavy as in deep summer—Moses pulls back from the touch he's simply taken for granted. He flushes and turns away, finding only: "Birds are taking their time today," as a way of hiding his embarrassment, and keeping a calculated distance from her.

Mag herself notices her own body's changes slowly, reluctantly, shocked one morning by drops of blood on her pantaloons, and examining her belly and thighs for a cut or insect bite, even though Peggy has warned that someday soon she'll find blood in her underwear or on her sheets, and shown her the rolls of bandages in the washroom cupboard and how to pin them around her hips. She hates the bulky cloth between her thighs, even as she learns how to secure it; hates the chafe as she runs and climbs trees ahead of Moses. She begins to drop behind those days of the month; Moses notices and teases: "You don't have to let me win." She can't explain, and simply turns away; soon she'll say she's not feeling well—and in fact she doesn't, more in her mind or spirit, than in her body, which carries its changes quite lightly.

Soon after, her chemise no longer fits smoothly over her chest; it's as if some force she hasn't felt or wanted has come to push up under her skin. Her dresses are so tight in the bodice that she thinks of binding her chest, but is embarrassed to ask Peggy or Lucy for a length of cloth. Both women notice her discomfort, though Peggy suggests off-handedly: "Let's see if any of Angelica's old dresses fit you, and, if not, we can sew you some new ones and chemises. You can pick fabrics from what we get for Angelica and Isba."

The Peale girls have seen the bloody pads soaking in the laundry tubs, and noted how her work dress stretches tight across her chest. Angelica tactfully acts as if nothing's different, but Isba teases when no adult is around: "Fell off the roof, did you?" to

Mag's bewilderment and dawning shame. "I didn't . . ." she begins, and even Angelica has to stifle a laugh.

The young boys begin to avoid her, even Moses, her faithful companion: racing, fishing, climbing, exploring. Charlie turns scarlet when she comes near him, and backs away as if she's contagious. The almost-men watch her with a new interest; she registers Raph's gaze as penetrating the thin cotton of her dress. Rembrandt is more subtle, appraising her lengthening neck, the angle of her cheekbones; he calculates how soon he can ask her to pose. Rubens has always paid her silent homage, baffled by his own attraction to her awkward grace, diverting it to his care for rabbits and moles wounded by his scythe, his delicate handling of growing plants. To Charles Willson, she's a point around which his worry circles, seeing her becoming a woman and wondering what will become of her; how long he can protect her from the world's cruelty and from his own sons.

Chapter 19

ELIZA IS QUERULOUS IN THE EARLY FALL HEAT, complaining that she can't find a comfortable way to sleep or even move. She wants only lemons to suck, and eats hardly any solid food, although Peggy cajoles and tries to tempt her with Lucy's most delicate custards and broths. Charles Willson teases: "How's my lemon girl?" but Eliza seems to know that his heart isn't in his jokes and gentle flirting. He remembers the girl he painted when he first met her: pale as if she'd never felt the sun, and adoring. Her first gift to him was a set of silver buttons for his best shirt, but he remembers too that she didn't offer to sew them on, and he had to persuade Peggy to do it.

He loved her voice when he first heard her singing with her friends, and thought it promised an appreciation of sensual pleasure, but her body under his was limp, almost as if she was asleep, or wanted to be. Not like Rachel, who would cry out in abandon and cling to him, even after twenty-eight years together, and who gave birth, year after year, to eleven children, six of whom lived to grow up.

As an old man, looking back on his life and taking up his "Pensil" to write about it, he will write to Jefferson that he spent too much time traveling and inventing machines to make his farm more efficient: the grain and cotton mills, the windmills and dams. Just as he never points out that Monticello has been built and is maintained by slave labor, or asks his friend about Sally Hemings, he never seems to wonder, except perhaps before his shaving mirror, why he, so eager to be "modern," hadn't tried to prevent pregnancy by other means than intermittent abstinence: why he has such a large household to support.

He rides to the city often in the days before Eliza's lying-in, with portrait commissions to fill, paints to buy, and, truth be told, eager to be away from a house filled with anxious waiting. Sometimes he takes Moses to carry his paint-case, his easel and rolls of canvas, and, on one of his trips, sees an exhibit of profile cuts, *silhouettes*, from France that the gallery owner promotes as an inexpensive way to take a likeness. When one prospective portrait sitter cancels for lack of money, Charles Willson asks—although he's never cut a profile before, if the man would like him to take a less costly, less time-consuming likeness of him and his wife. "I've never done this before, so I won't charge you anything unless you like it, and then, whatever you choose."

With heavy black paper, sharp pencil, scissors, and a sharp eye for faces, Charles Willson has two sitters that day instead of one. After the task of reproducing the weight and shape of each feature for a painting, let alone finding the right colors, to trace a profile on paper is the work of a moment. The artist's hand has to be steady in the tracing and the cutting, and Charles Willson's is; the first sitters pay more than he thinks he deserves, and a business begins. Moses, too, has an attentive eye and a steady hand. Charles Willson makes him practice alongside him, often finding the boy's work more accurate and more expressive than his own.

"When you're twenty-six, you can make a living doing this, and be free," Charles Willson tells him, loading canvases, paints, and black card stock into the chaise. "Until then, you'll keep what you earn from the profiles you cut. You have a gift." Moses, holding the easel, thinks, *I'm an artist.*

Charles Willson teaches his sons and Charlie to cut profiles too, but Moses has the greatest aptitude, often drawing hair and collars on the profiles with India ink to make each likeness more distinct. More than one sitter balks when Charles Willson introduces Moses as: "My man here who'll do a better job for you than I can."

"He's just a boy, and a Black one besides," the customer argues. "I don't want him looking at my wife and daughters." Charles Willson bridles his tongue but still answers sharply: "You'll have to wait until next week, when I have time for you." The man decides to wait.

Mag will ask Charles Willson, one day in his library when he wakes from his nap to find her reading or writing there: "Why doesn't Moses have painting lessons like the rest of us, even me?"

It's a question art historians and scholars will ask, sometimes accusingly, some sympathetically, and one he now answers pragmatically: "He's much more likely to make a living cutting profiles than painting portraits. And he needs to make a living to be free."

Profile-cutting is so popular, in these years before Daguerre's invention, and Charles Willson becomes so tired of lugging his painting cases from farm to borrowed spaces in the city that he asks Gloriana—whom he visits more, she teases, as a rental agent—if she knows an empty building to house his cutting materials and paints:

"So you tire of farming?" she asks, refilling his wine glass. "The great agrarian ideal fails to satisfy?"

He frowns, struggling to keep from saying something he wants to keep hidden, especially from Eliza, who finds life on the farm trying, even though its work is almost entirely done for her and kept from her. She would, he thinks, seize on the smallest complaint as a reason to move back to the city, and never let the subject alone until he acquiesced.

"Ahh . . . no; it's more that I need the city, need to take up my pencil again, need to have space to paint and show paintings in. I like to have people coming in. . ."

"You like impressing them."

"Yes, and with farming, you never know when you're done, or if anyone thinks you've done well, and with crops, you never know what will take hold. Or what weather will do."

"Not to mention the help or lack of it." She's heard much from him on this topic before.

He goes on, forgetting that he's trod this path too often. "Yes, and the expense and lack of reliability. Thomas doesn't realize how lucky he is."

"To be a slave master? What about *his* workers?'

"They're treated well," he says, but has lowered his head and can't look at her.

"I can't believe you said that!" Gloriana rises abruptly, and, as she does, the wine decanter tips over. Both she and Charles Willson stare at the red river flowing across the table and onto her white skirts a moment before she rings the small bell for her maid.

"Marie, please flood it with cold water, the way you do with blood," she says. She turns toward her bedroom without looking at him, and he understands it's time for him to go. As his hand is on the knob, she calls after him: "Any plans for them yet?" meaning Scar and Lucy. And then, softening," I'll see what I can do about a painting room for you."

"I would be most grateful," he answers.

The more Eliza complains, the more Charles Willson plans to take time away. He tries to secure help for her, but Mrs. DePeyster is insulted to be asked: "as if I were a common servant," she sniffs to her husband. She and her daughter have never been close, and, cordial as the DePeysters are to Charles Willson, they're disappointed in Eliza for falling in love with a middle-aged, never-solvent artist, talented though he may be.

Charles Willson satisfies his sense of responsibility by enlisting Peggy, Lucy, and Mag, who promise to help as much as they can, but without enthusiasm. He charges Rembrandt and Rubens—not bothering with Raph—with riding for the midwife, Yarrow's Antigua, as soon as they're called.

He takes Moses with him on most of his journeys, always now to "Philada," as he calls it, and once to Charleston to see the museum of natural history there. Does he feel more impressive, more respected by curators and collectors, with this well-dressed, handsome young Black boy in attendance? He will hardly admit to more than teaching Moses the ways of art and commerce, or possibly needing the boy's help taking notes, keeping track of important papers, carrying painting cases, but would never acknowledge enjoying a slave owner's privilege.

When friends and acquaintances hear that Charles Willson plans to expand his painting rooms into a museum, they begin to send him things from their hunts and explorations: dead birds and animals, snakes and snakeskins, rocks, stones, shells and sea creatures. Some he must refuse—when the smell of death fills the hallway—but with his usual determination and confidence to enact whatever he sets his mind to, he apprentices himself to a master taxidermist in New York, letting Eliza know with an offhand: "I'll need to be in New York for a few weeks." And at her protests: "Peggy, Lucy, Mag, and the girls can give you help enough. The boys know where the midwife lives."

"I don't want Lucy touching me," she throws at his back.

"Her food is good enough for you, though," he retorts.

Chapter 20

AS A STUDENT, RELIEVED of his usual responsibilities, Charles Willson learns to slit rabbits' skin so deftly he can remove them in one piece, slide the bloody organs out, scrape the smelly evidence away, dry the interiors just enough to be pliable, fill the once-living bodies with cotton, and sew them up again. The eyes popped out, the sockets are filled with marbles from the glass-blower's wand; the animals' claws, noses, and foot-pads he sculpts from a mixture of leather and gutta percha. Absorbed in these tasks, happy to be moving closer to his vision, he's sorry to take leave of his fellow museum-builders and take the packet back to Philadelphia.

On the farm, he finds that Eliza hasn't slept: her huge belly makes every position unbearable. She raises her head with the despair of a woman who knows she's the least of a man's concerns. "I'm here now," he says, gripping her shoulder so hard she winces in dismay; with her silence, he whirls away to his projects.

He designates Moses the chief taxidermist, choosing the least decayed specimens that have accumulated in his absence to begin his lessons. Faster, with smaller, more flexible fingers than Charles Willson's, Moses is soon skinning and stuffing squirrels, rabbits, and birds that he and the Peale boys shoot on the farm, and injecting them with a tincture of mercury to keep the maggots away.

It takes two men, sweating and cursing, to lift the box from the stage, which has stopped in front of the house in a swirl of dust.

"Where to, sir?" one asks Charles Willson, who is, luckily, on his way out the front door. Thinking it's a crate of shrimp he's ordered, he waves them through the hall toward the kitchen, but Peggy shouts, "What's next? We've already got enough shrimp for two nights of parties!"

"This is too heavy for shrimps, Ma'am," the stagecoach driver mutters between clenched teeth. "We'll just set it here," meaning the long deal table, now filled with just-picked greens, which he pushes unceremoniously aside. "We should be paid extra for jobs like this," he says, straightening and arching his back. "With all due respect, sir," he wipes his forehead and looks intently at Charles Willson, who fumbles in his waistcoat pocket for coins, not enough to please the driver and his helper, but adequate to receive the manifest that reads: SAMPLES FROM THE MISSISSIPPI SHORE COLLECTED BY YR FRIEND M. LEWIS HEARD YOU MIGHT HAVE A USE FOR THESE.

Prying up the protesting lid, Charles Willson finds a jumble of newspaper, and inside, shells, stones, fish skeletons; and is stopped by Peggy:

"Take your toys somewhere else, Charles Willson: out of my clean kitchen!"

No one else in the household dares speak to him this way, and there's no one else he'd obey. "Rubens!" he yells in the direction of the kitchen garden, "Rubens, I need your help!" But before his son can lend his sturdy shoulder to this task, Moses is at Charles Willson's elbow: "I can take one end."

Shuffling, the weight unbalanced by their uneven heights, the man and the boy edge to the side room, the mudroom, where boots and heavy coats are kept. As they begin to unpack and unwrap, they quickly run out of room on the small side table. Charles Willson wants to clean and catalog each specimen: oyster shells, rocks imprinted with the shapes of ferns and of animal paws; a broken triangle of pottery, burnt sienna with a black band. "There needs to be a new museum, with cases for all this."

And so, in spite of Eliza's protests that he'll always be in the city, he searches for a building large enough to contain his vision; he follows every lead, from warehouse to abandoned mansion, until he hears the magic rumor, second-hand from one of Gloriana's clients: *The second floor of the new Town Hall may be let rent-free.*

They fill what will be the Long Room with buckets of lime and long-handled brushes, ladders and drop-cloths, when a woman with a worry-streaked face knocks on the door-frame: "Mr. Peale?"

He hates to be interrupted in a task, but wipes his brush and tries to arrange his expression into the model of genial acceptance he aspires to: "Ma'am?"

"Do you have work for my daughter? I heard you were teaching some to cut profiles, sir."

"My sons and Moses here, yes, and my nieces. When we're settled in here, I'll send word," and she leaves a card, the lettering overlaid with the image of a flower, its center inscribed with tiny letters. The name *Honeywell* snags something in Charles Willson's memory that he can't quite place, but Moses remembers: "That's the girl with no hands and only one foot. . ."

"And that with only three toes," Charles Willson adds. "I don't see how she can cut profiles."

"Just lose the card," Raph says. "We have enough people to help as it is," with a pointed glance at Moses, who picks up his paintbrush and doesn't take the bait, knowing he's of more help than Raph, and earns, too, more of Charles Willson's praise.

When Martha herself comes, the Long Room is finished: the

cabinets along its walls half-filled with specimens, the tables set with scissors and black papers, light streaming from the long windows at each end. A young man carries her up the stairs and looks around for a place to set her down. Rembrandt and Raph stand aside in embarrassment, but their father moves forward with greetings: "Come in, come in! Will this chair be all right?" pushing a ladder-back close to her. "Or will you be more comfortable on the floor? Moses, there must be a small rug in the office. . ."

At first, she watches as the young men and Moses trace Angelica's profile onto white sketching paper, cut out the shape, and trace it onto black. Charles Willson works freehand, drawing directly onto the black; he demonstrates what long practice of seeing and limning makes possible. He wouldn't tell Martha what to do, even if he knew how to guide her.

She must figure out how to hold the scissors and wield them: paper grasped by her toes, one scissor handle in her mouth, the other pushed by the stump of her toe-less leg. She bends her body like a pretzel and holds her pose steady for the time it takes to catch the likeness. Even when Charles Willson brings the physiognotrace with its mechanical tracing arm, she cuts by mouth.

People pay well for the images of themselves that fall from her foot, and for satisfying their curiosity as they watch her perform. One of the first things she buys with her earnings is a silver ring for her biggest toe, which gleams as the scissors flash, and attracts young men, making Mag jealous when Moses describes it.

Moses himself has become a star, dressed in a turban made from one of Angelica's scarves and a paisley cape that was a piano cover: a warrior prince from no country but one Charles Willson has imagined. He's charged with standing at the museum's street door, calling, "Profiles cut here! Your likeness cheap, Ladies and Gentlemen!" He himself will run upstairs to be the cutter, whipping off his costume, following the lamplit shapes of his sitters with a fine knife until the black paper falls away, as his sitters stay

still, entranced by the novelty of having a Black boy make something so delicate and true. For an extra fee, he'll add bits of hair
or a collar or necklace or frill, adding up his earnings each week,
wondering how to ask Charles Willson when he can be free.

New specimens are as plentiful as customers: The heron has been
shot through the throat in flight; there's only a bead of blood on
the drift of gray feathers that flutter as Charles Willson pulls
the bird from the hunter's sack. Here in the Taxidermy Room,
he'll show Moses how to use the sharpest knife to cut down from
beak to belly, and slide the skin and feathered coat from the bird's
body. He lifts out the pink heart and bulbous lungs, the crop and
stomach sac still filled with fish from the bird's last swoop over
the water.

He'll ask Moses to help him burn every part that was most
alive in the dooryard burn pit, and set the bones and feathers out
to dry. The smell is terrible on taxidermy days, but no more so
than the back-alley outhouses give out in the humid air. There's
room now to let the bones dry but still be flexible, to arrange
them so the heron will fly over the specimen cases in the Long
Room: wings spread wide, legs drawn up to its chest.

"Or we can show it swooping. . .if a big fish comes in, we
can make a pond for it under the bird." Charles Willson makes
it child's play, this particular art, and Moses is his best student,
the one he'll choose for this work, even when his sons—to their
dismay—aren't traveling or painting.

"It will be the star of the Long Room." Charles Willson exults
in the space filled with glass-fronted cases to keep out dust, mice
and maggots; and with side rooms for storing, dissecting, stuffing, sewing, lettering, display-stand constructing: all the hidden
work behind the exhibits. In one of his last self-portraits, he will
be an imposing figure, pulling up a curtain to reveal the Long
Room's wonders, as if he's a stand-in for God, showing off all

His creation. He will try, without success but with unwavering belief, to persuade public officials, from Jefferson to the City of Philadelphia, to support the museum he's built for the public's edification. Is it, as some critics suggest, that the citizens of the new country are bent only on making money; or is it that the objects in his museum are too ordinary: the creatures, stones and shells people see every day? Or is it that they don't want to be reminded of their own inattention?

Chapter 21

O NE FALL MORNING when Charles Willson enters the stable, he finds Scar seated on a tack-box mending a bridle. Since Scar's arm has healed, since Charles Willson's fall into grief and his struggle out of it, building the museum with a desperate energy, the two men—both tall, one Black, without an extra ounce of flesh; the other white, flushed pink, a bit thick around the middle and in the jowls—face each other differently. Where once he would have stood at Charles Willson's entrance, Scar now merely nods, "Good morning," and continues to work the leather for a new customer.

Instead of asking Scar to bring the trap around—he's taking Moses into the city with him again—Charles Willson wheels the carriage out and starts for the freshest horse's stall; then pauses: "We should talk, Scar."

"Of course, whenever you want." He's been omitting to add *Sir* for weeks now. The young men speak openly to him, not their father; Raph mocks Charles Willson cleverly and viciously; Scar doesn't agree or admonish, but listens with a noncommittal smile that encourages confidences, before saying mildly: "If you stopped drinking your father's liquor and eating his food, he might go easier on you."

Slipping a bridle over the horse's ears now, and pulling its fore-lock through, Charles Willson sets the time, although he phrases it as a question: "Tonight, after Lucy finishes washing up?"

If Charles Willson were talking business with a neighbor, he would bring out a flagon of the best hard cider and small glasses; he does so now, and pours for Lucy and Scar. In spite of the time of relative freedom they've known here, they can't help feeling and showing their discomfort. Scar takes the glass set out for him so slowly that Charles Willson asks: "Are you still having pain?"

Scar doesn't say what he's thinking: *I always thought a knife would stop my arm.* "No, it's just stiff; Yarrow sent some salve that we rub on it," he answers, glancing at Lucy to include her. She sits, straight and tense, on the edge of her chair.

By not breaking state laws, and Charles Willson will uninten-tionally break this family. "I can free you and Lucy," he says to Scar, thinking Lucy may dissolve in tears if he looks at her. "You both will be able to support yourselves in the city. Moses will need to stay here with us until he's twenty-six."

As Lucy's composure cracks, he rushes on: "He's a great pro-file-cutter already; he can keep all he earns from that. In a few years" he minimizes the length—"when he's manumitted"—he can't say, *when I set him free*—"he'll have some money saved."

"But," Scar says, taking a long drink of the cider, which burns his throat, "he'll be with you, not his family." Lucy looks at him in alarm, but Charles Willson doesn't take offense. "You can visit, he can visit. We'll take good care of him."

There's a pause into which the promise drops. Almost as uneasy as they, Charles Willson leaps over the abyss: "Both of you are well-equipped to make your way. Scar, your saddle-making got known throughout Germantown; as soon as we put out the word that you're in business, the custom will come back. And Lucy, your cooking is so fine that I'll hate to see you go."

Although he hasn't taken a drink of alcohol since his last

confrontation with Raph, Charles Willson pours himself a glass of the cider. "We'll have to make sure your saddles are flying out the door before I can in conscience manumit you."

"How long are you thinking?" Scar gets straight to the point Charles Willson is avoiding.

"As long as it takes." He takes another, longer drink.

"I think with Lucy's cooking, we can do just fine until the broken saddles find their way to me." Scar speaks casually, as if what he's asserting is of no importance, then bends slightly forward. "Do you have the papers with you?"

Charles Willson gets up abruptly, a bit light-headed from the cider. "I'll have to get Moses to fetch them." This conversation hasn't gone quite as he'd planned; he feels somehow remiss, diminished, as he makes his grand gesture, not having realized that there's no nobility in it.

Lucy speaks for the first time since they've gathered at the kitchen table, and with surprising firmness: "First, Scar and I have to talk to Moses."

That night, as dark closes in, a sound comes from the playhouse— deep, plaintive, struck on a groundhog-gut string stretched across the gourd Scar had found and dried, like the one his father had, now lost somewhere: tossed or broken or left behind after one removal after another. He'd set aside the biggest of the big gourds he'd picked, scraped the bowl of its flesh, and brought it to the kitchen as usual, to be mashed and baked. When Moses had asked why the shell sat on the south windowsill, and Lucy had watched with a knowing smile, Scar had simply answered,

"Wait and see. "

When it was dry but not brittle, he'd stretched a groundhog skin and strings of groundhog guts across the opening, and attached a scrap-wood neck. "When it's safe," he'd answered, and then, after the shooting: "When I have reason."

Now he strums and tightens the strings; the tune he remembers carries the tone of joy mixed with sorrow that seems right for this night: this mixture of elation and pain ringing out against a night that shows nothing, gives no certainty.

Mag, carrying food scraps to the pigs that evening, hears a sound she thinks is a voice, except that there are no words and it's unlike any human sound she knows, and unlike any animal's: a song of earth, dark as the earth where the dead are buried; dark as earth where seeds come to life.

After she throws the cucumber peels, the lettuce stems and potato skins over the fence and the pigs have come running to her *Dinner, dinner!* and she's scratched a neck or two as they bend to eat, she moves closer to the playhouse door. As she stands in the shadow listening, thinking she's not been seen, Moses catches sight of her and runs forward.

"Come in, come in!" Without hesitation he takes not her good hand, but the fingerless one she usually keeps hidden, and pulls her into the circle of lamplight.

Lucy makes room for her on the settle; Scar, bent over his instrument, making it sing, doesn't notice her. For Moses, this is the moment that joins his future to Mag's; for her, the only thing that enters her consciousness is the sound the banjo makes. The question that will preoccupy her, as she kneads bread and wrings out the sheets, peels and chops the vegetables Rubens brings from the garden, scalds the dinner plates with boiling water, is how to put words together to make such a music, or something *like* that music. Something not like the sounds she finds in Phillis Wheatley's book, although she loves how firmly the lines thump and make her feel like a soldier raising a flag.

Somewhere in the damp darkness, the notes catch other ears: Ira Shaw and Jeb Smith returning from a habitual errand, this time leading a man behind Jeb's horse, a rope tied to his neck. Jeb pulls up hard on his horse's bridle; the man he's dragging bangs his head against its broad rump.

"Hear that?" he asks Shaw. "Sounds like a slave tune to me."

"That's Peale's place, you fool. We don't have business there," Shaw answers, spurring his horse. "We need to get to Philadelphia with this cargo; I don't want to ride all night."

Disappointed, humiliated by Shaw as always, Smith takes his anger out on the horse and the man behind him, slashing with his whip, jerking his captive so the man falls and is dragged along the road until Shaw shouts: "Stop, fool! We get paid only if we bring him in alive."

In the playhouse filled with music, light, and a family's breath, no one hears the hoofbeats or saddle-creak as the slavers quicken their pace, moving away toward the highway. Only Argus raises his head and stares at Scar, who stops playing: "What is it, friend?" The dog, mostly ignored as the Peale children have grown older, adopted Scar in his convalescence, scarcely leaving his chair in the kitchen and alerting him when anyone approached. They have the relationship of comrades, much like Scar's with the horses he trains and cares for: not as master and animal to be mastered, but as fellow beings.

Argus stays at attention, his nose twitching slightly, his ears raised as much as a retriever's can. Scar goes to the open door and listens to the dark, which gives the faint whiff of horse dung that hadn't been there before. He catches no sound or other scent, and stands for a minute to be sure he's not deceiving himself. When he picks up his instrument again, the music celebrates the quiet of the night, the home he and Lucy have made. Lucy now puts her arm around Moses, and pulls tight.

She'd held back tears when she and Scar told him they were leaving but would see him "all the time." Moses, thinking of Mag, reassures her: "I'll be just fine here. Every year I'll be closer to twenty-six."

"We'll be counting the days," his mother says. "We won't forget your birthday."

Chapter 22

"**Y**OU KEEP MOVING, DAMN YOU!**" Rembrandt throws down his brush, and Raph laughs: "You're not fast enough." One of the lessons Charles Willson has set them is taking a quick likeness: "*The busier the sitter, the less time he'll have for sitting.*" He doesn't have to say that those busiest men are the customers they most want, not always because they pay the most—often they don't—but because their portraits will bring the painters the most prominence.

Rembrandt can sit still for hours in front of his family's easels, but Raph is restless, both because he can't help moving and because he wants to subvert his father's teaching and his siblings' obedience. The portrait Rembrandt finishes shows Raph half-turned away, lips parted, his shirt collar open, his hair mussed as if by wind. Rembrandt has incorporated his brother's wish for flight into the paint, working from what he knows of him, not just what he sees in front of him. His father, surveying the finished work, feels a prick of dismay along with pride; *The boy has surpassed me,* he'll write to Jefferson.

He anoints the painting with his highest praise: "It's a speaking likeness." He'll send Rembrandt and Raph to Charleston, Savannah, and New Orleans to fulfill commissions in his place;

as he ages, and as the farm needs more attention, he can't accept every offer.

Mag, finishing her writing lesson, catches sight of Raph's face on the easel and catches her breath; it's as if he's *there*, not rushing up the stairs to pack his valise for the journey south. He doubles back into the painting room to get the scarf he pulled off during the sitting and nods to Mag, who is silenced even more by his actual presence than by his likeness.

"Want to help me pack?" That Mag is no longer a skinny girl hasn't escaped the older boys' attention; for his part, Raph has noticed her eyes on him a bit longer than necessary or usual, and been amused by the blush she tries to hide when he comes on her unexpectedly.

Now she follows him as he sprints up the stairs, heart pounding so loud she's sure he can hear it. The bedroom he shares with Rembrandt is a mess of linens, jackets, stockings, waistcoats, knee-pants, and an open valise. "I don't know what to take," he shrugs, with an air of helplessness intended to induce Mag to make the choices for him, but she is too caught by the scent of his bedclothes—faint sweat mixed with lavender—to speak, let alone make a suggestion.

With a slight laugh, he moves past her to close the door. He twists the lock and turns to her, putting his hands on her shoulders and pushing one leg between both of hers. It's easy, startled as she is, to tip her backwards onto the bed; it's his brother's that will be soiled, not his own. He puts his mouth on hers, hard, forcing her lips open, and, holding her against the mattress with one hand, begins to pull at her clothes.

Shocked, as her blouse tears, she begins to push back, her years of hard work, tree-climbing, running, coming to help her. On her side, too, is Raph's own lack of experience; in the future, his seductions will be skillful, subtle, and successful.

Now Mag turns her head to the side and struggles to reach his ear; distracted by her skirt and apron's resistance, he lets go her mouth and one arm. She's able to reach the gold pirate's ring in his ear lobe and pulls with her strong teeth. She feels the blood on her own throat before he screams and jumps up: "Fuck fuck FUCK! Look what you've done!" Her dress is soaked red, as are Rembrandt's sheets and some linens he'd tossed there.

Raph holds a pillow to his bleeding ear. "Find my earring, bitch!" But Mag runs to unlock the door. "Find it yourself!" He takes her by the arm as she's halfway to the stairs. "You'll say you had a nosebleed while you were helping me pack." He dares her to protest, with an intensity stronger than any declaration of love.

"No, I'll say you did," she answers, running to her room to strip off her dress and find a clean one. The laundry will take an especially long time, getting the childbirth treatment: hours of soaking in salted water.

Scar brings the trap to the door where Charles Willson has been waiting with his paints, profile papers, and portfolio; he'll drop his sons at the packet boat and spend a few days in the city. He suspects that the Slave Patrol isn't far away; it's not safe for Scar to be abroad by himself, even with the new papers in his vest.

"Boys! It's time to go!" Rembrandt winces at being a *Boy* as he's called on to do his father's work; Raph snorts in derision, having expected nothing more. They clatter down the stairs, greatcoats flying. As he passes Mag, who stands unmoving in the hall, Raph ducks to scrape her cheek with his lips: "Be good, darling," and climbs into the trap beside his brother.

Rubens, who has left the garden to see them off, also sees Mag lift her hand to her cheek where Raph's lips have brushed it. She watches the cloud of dust that swirls after the trap until it's out of sight. Rubens notices the curve of her neck and the curls of neck-hairs tied up off it shaking a little; he would touch her thin shoulder if he could, if he thought she wouldn't shake

off his hand. In the garden he pulls weeds with a speed and violence that startles him; he stops when a potato plant dripping
dirt comes out of the ground in his hands. Peggy, who's come
to the garden fence to ask for his help carrying the heavy wet
sheets to the mangle, says gently, "After you help me, Rube, why
don't you take the day off?"

She doesn't ask Mag to help, but pours extra salt and cold
water on the blood-soaked sheets and stirs them in the wash-pot.
To Mag, she says: "Girl, you can watch the bread today; I'll tend
to this." Mag starts from the waking dream she's entered, and sees
that Peggy, who notices almost everything on the farm, hasn't
missed anything she might hope to hide. As she turns toward
the pantry, Peggy addresses her back, speaking so low that Mag
hardly hears her: "If you need to ask me anything, tell me anything, you can. Just don't give your heart to that one."

Her heart, though, is already gone: on the road, on the packet
boat, in the wind that rakes Raph's hair. Feeling still the force of
his body, telling herself he needs her, checking the bread's swell
under its towel, taking in its sharp, live scent, she takes up the pen
and notebook she keeps on a pantry shelf.

If you could turn back and see me there, she writes,
I would put my heart in your pocket
so it would always be with you —
I don't need it, except as it's yours

She's not sure this is all she wants to say, or even *if* this is what
she means, but Lucy has come into the pantry—"Eliza's time is
near"—and she doesn't want anyone to see her writing, as if writing is kind of laziness, an act useful only to oneself. She blots the
shimmering words and stoppers the inkwell. "Peggy's stirring the
wash. I'll run get her."

Eliza screams when Peggy tries to put a pillow under her pelvis, and screams with every contraction, so furiously that no one can stand to be near her for long. Peggy and Mag take turns holding her damp hand and washing her feverish face. When Angelica and Isba come with fresh cloths and basins of cool water, Peggy pulls Angelica aside, whispering, not quite under her breath: "Has Rubens gone for Antigua?" Angelica, fifteen and horrified by Eliza's writing and screaming, shakes her head, unable to speak.

"Good God, why not?" Peggy pushes the girl out of her way and runs to the garden, where Rubens drops the beets he's been pulling and heads for the stable.

Antigua lives only on the next farm, but it takes Rubens over an hour to find and bring her into the birthing room. Not young, but still supple enough to ride astride, she holds Rubens around the waist as he urges his horse to a gallop. Eliza's screams reach them before they reach the dooryard; Antigua dismounts before Rubens has reined in his winded horse, and runs inside. When she comes to Eliza's tangled bed with her midwife's herbs and sure hands, Eliza screams again, not in pain, but anger at the sight of her: "Don't touch me, bitch!"

Mag, whose turn it is to bathe Eliza's face and hold her hand, turns and calls for Peggy, who addresses Eliza with furious authority: "Antigua is the midwife, Miss, who birthed all the Peale children on this farm, and will deliver you of this one!"

Eliza simply shudders and begins to sob. Mag, seeing the thin young body, its belly so distended and pulsing, curl up like a small child, can't help feeling a grudging pity, and wonders why Charles Willson isn't here, and why Eliza's mother and sisters haven't come. Antigua's hand is on her shoulder: "Steep these in boiling water and bring the tankard back to me." She hasn't noticed that Mag is missing a hand, or has noticed and ignores it, bending to Eliza, murmuring softly without a shade of rancor: "Let me help you, and the baby will come out fine."

Eliza turns her awkward bulk as far away in the bed as she can, and keeps sobbing, but more quietly now.

Her screams, too, change in timbre, becoming less frequent and at the same time deeper, less unbearable to hear. She takes the tea that Mag has brewed and that Antigua holds to her cracked lips. Toward dusk she gives one last anguished groan, as if her insides are being torn from her body, and, in a sense, they are: as the baby's head crowns between her legs and his slippery bloody shape slips onto the rumpled sheet. Antigua reaches for the small knife in its pouch at her waist and cuts the umbilical cord; there will be bathing and stanching, and more herbs to stop the bleeding.

The baby begins to cry in Peggy's arms, the first thrilling cries of being alive, just as Charles Willson comes from his business in the city. "A boy! He'll be our next Titian!" he declares, bending to kiss Eliza's tear-streaked cheek and turning away without waiting to hear a reply.

Peggy, standing in the doorway, looks at him askance; he answers without her having to say a word: "I was hoping the ink would dry," and he's on his way downstairs, pulling off his jacket as he goes.

In the kitchen, Moses has untied the bulging portfolio and begun to spread the profiles on the work table for Mag to see, before Charles Willson comes to admonish: "No, no: these go in the Painting Room." And then, as Moses moves to gather up the thick pieces: "Best to carry them one by one and tack them up; the ink's not quite dry on your additions." Black curves and ripples shimmer and tremble here and there on the surfaces in the woodstove's heat: likenesses of landowners and their wives, carefully eliding the most offending wattles but taking nothing away from a prominent nose.

Moses has added a ruffle, a bow or ascot's fold, a wavy

strand of hair or a mustache curl that pleases the sitters. When the ink is completely dry, he'll unpin each sheet and begin to work from memory. When she has a free moment, Mag sits at the painting table across from him, her chin propped against her partial hand, watching him dip the narrowest pen in the inkwell, scrape it of excess ink and re-trace the delicate lines. Charles Willson has taught Raph and Rembrandt to cut profiles too, but they—and he himself—are too impatient to add what they call *mere decoration*, and too eager to move on to portrait commissions, for the income and prestige they can bring.

Mag sits almost dreaming as the lines flow smoothly: straight ones and curving, from Moses' hand. She loves the silence around them and his absorption that doesn't ask for her approval, or even acknowledge her presence, but that she knows depends upon it. When Lucy calls from the kitchen, "Where are you, Mag? I need help with the chickens," Mag starts as if from sleep, and pushes herself away from the painting table without answering, not wanting to break Moses' concentration. Later, after lunch has been made, carried to table and cleared away, she'll find Charles Willson asleep in the library, and sits near him until he stirs, eyeglasses slipping down his nose: "How are you this afternoon, Mag?" as if he hadn't been napping, but is in full control. "How did you like the book I lent you?"

She's been copying Shakespeare's sonnets and has some by heart, but her feeling outruns her ability to speak. "I love it; thank you, sir." If Charles Willson has expected a more articulate response, he doesn't betray any disappointment:

"I have something new from England called *Lyrical Ballads*," and hands her Wordsworth. "Let me know what you think." He with his *Biographica Litteraria*, she with the *Ballads*, they read quietly together and apart in the quiet room, until a slight lessening of the afternoon light and a noise from the hall let her know that Rubens has come with his basket full of vegetables for dinner.

Rising to leave with her finger marking her place, she takes this moment before Peggy or Lucy can call her: "Sir, Moses has such a fine hand for profiles, why don't you teach him to paint?"

"Has he ever complained to you? He's never said anything to me."

"No sir," she falters and blushes, wondering if she's been too bold.

In another household., a servant—and a young girl at that—would be reprimanded or worse, but Charles Willson prides himself on his egalitarianism: "When Moses is free, he'll need to make a living. Profile-cutting will be much more practical for him than painting portraits." Because Mag seems to expect, and deserve, more explanation, and forgetting how young she is, he adds: "As it is, some of my customers complain when they find a Black boy will cut their profile. I have to point out that they won't be looking at him; they'll be facing to the side. I vouch for his skill, and, if they insist on having me, I raise their price."

Slipping soldier beans from their shells, she wonders why people would complain that Moses is sitting in the same room with them, with his thick black paper and profile-cutting knife, or why they wouldn't want him opposite them, with his deep dark eyes and gold-brown skin that she often compares to the maple dining table that she cleans and polishes it so it glows. Moses himself, no dream, comes to the kitchen, his profile-embellishing done, and in his exuberance reaches into the bowl she's filling with beans. Laughing, she smacks his hand; the rust-red globes roll onto the kitchen floor.

"Moses!" Lucy says, more sharply that she means to: "Pick them up!" and he crawls after them over the knotty floorboards.

"It was *my* fault,' Mag admits, and, taking a smaller bowl to gather the strays, drops to her knees beside him.

Not for the first time, Lucy notices that they act as one, and wonders what the future will hold for these no-longer children; what place they may find in this world that doesn't welcome his color or her imperfection.

Rubens, coming in with his hat full of beets, notices them, too: Mag and Moses bumping into each other in their hunt for stray beans and laughing, laughing at their collisions, like the children they were only a year or two before.

To Rubens, there's nothing funny here; he almost hurls the beets with their dirt-filled roots onto the scrubbed work table. "Rube! Come back here and clean up your mess!" Peggy scolds, as if he too were still a child and she had some authority over him, but he has stormed out, and won't come back for dinner.

Finding Scar in the stable yard cleaning tack, he starts to snarl, "Shouldn't you be. . ." and falters, not knowing what to reprimand Scar for, except for being Moses' father, for *being there*, in his way. Scar, rubbing tallow into the leather, regards Rubens with mild interest. He has noticed Rubens' small attentions to Mag: the glistening tooth of new garlic beside her dinner plate; the bunch of wild violets in a jelly jar by her station at the sink.

"Need your horse?" he asks now, as if there were nothing unusual about Rubens going somewhere in the middle of a work day with his shirt pulled out of his britches and no jacket on.

"No, no," Rubens mumbles, not sure where he means to go or what he wants to do. "Sorry to have bothered you," and heads back to the garden, stumbling over a pail and not stopping to right it. He wants away from there, or away from himself. If he had been Raph, he would have taken a bottle of wine from their father's cellar. Rembrandt would never have gotten himself so ensnared.

Chapter 23

His brothers return from the south in a clatter of hooves, gravel, and male energy, whooping: "Rube! Charlie! Moses! Come carry our trunks!" Raph is carrying two bottles of rum in his valise, along with soiled shirts that he tosses to Mag with a mocking "For you, sweetheart!" that she wants to hear as if he'd thrown her a bouquet, not these wine-soaked, sweat-stained linens. Rembrandt carries a wallet full of coins and paper money that he empties onto the kitchen table. "Where's Charles Willson?" He stopped calling Charles Willson *Father* when he undertook the commissions his father has no time for.

"What makes you think money belongs on my clean table, Rem?" Peggy confronts him, pride mixing with her indignation. He scoops up the bright-colored bills and glittering coins, and kisses her on the cheek. "You should see New Orleans and taste the food." Peggy pokes his mid-section where it bulges against his shirt: "I can see you did some tasting, young man."

To celebrate their return and the birth of their new brother—*Titian II*, their father wants everyone to call him—Raph and Rembrandt propose a party, even though Eliza, whom their father insists all her stepchildren call *Mother*, has kept to her bedroom since the birth. Mag and Angelica bring her meals; Anna on the Randolphs' farm has taken the baby to live with her and her own nursing child. Eliza had handed the fretful bundle over, seeing the slender brown woman bare her breast and hold Titian to it—pink skin on plum—with tearful relief. Small searching mouth to erect nipple, the baby attaches himself and stills in contentment.

"Don't worry, ma'am; he'll be fine." Eliza only sobs: at her own helplessness and incompetence; she's happy, in a way she can never tell anyone, not to hear the querulous crying, crying that her own small supply of milk can't satisfy.

Charles Willson stops in to see her in the evenings, invariably asking: "Feeling better? Feeling better?" as if by asking, he can make it so. Her weakness annoys him, to tell the truth: a reminder of his own powerlessness. Rachel would rouge her face and dress up to please him, even after losing their first daughter, and he would hold her tear-stained face against his shirt, after painting her in *The Abyss of Grief*, which some of his contemporaries deplore for being sentimental.

He sketches in the outlines of his new son's portrait most of the morning of the celebration; he's asked Anna to dress the baby in the long white dress that would be called the "christening dress," if this family believed in christenings. Titian himself stays still only a moment out of his nurse's arms before beginning to toss and fret, as Anna sings just above speech: *Hush, little baby, don't you cry.* Charles Willson works quickly, and from the memory of other babies; he wants to display the portrait at the party. Raph, coming into the painting room with a bottle he tries to hide from his father, mocks: "Trying to be Velasquez?" Charles Willson, absorbed, lets the taunt roll against him and fall way.

There will be a dance for Raph, Rembrandt, and Titian, with a buffet supper on the side. Peggy has lobbied hard not to make and serve a sit-down dinner in this warm fall weather and with the strain of caring for Eliza. The French doors in the gallery and drawing room let in the coming evening as Angelica takes her place at the harpsichord and Isba tests her flute's keys, Rubens tunes his violin with ear-splitting screeches at first, accustoming his dirt-stained hands to this different task; Moses brings the viola to his chin, thrilled at the way it thrums against his shoulder. Candles flutter to the movements Peggy, Lucy, and Mag make, carrying the platters of roast pig and scalloped oysters, roast potatoes and bitter greens dressed in oil and vinegar to the sideboards along the wall.

The music rises, tentative at first, as the guests arrive, and becomes more assured: reel, gavotte: the dancers line up with Raph at the head of one group, and Rembrandt at the other. The young women from the neighboring farms, and even from Philadelphia, wear their glistening silken best; their hair is pulled up high and tight, escaping ringlets dangling like bunches of grapes. Their jewelry, mostly borrowed from mothers and older sisters, catches the candlelight as they curtsy and whirl. Raph, who has taken several glasses of rum before the party officially began, calls instructions and greetings to old friends and new with an exuberance that makes his younger brothers wince with varying degrees of embarrassment: Rubens lowering his head to his instrument, Rembrandt covering his discomfort with a practiced formality.

Such a stick, one of the visiting girls whispers to another, who says: *But his brother . . .* as Raph whirls, his ponytail whipping behind him, his color high. They aren't the only young women caught by his beauty and energy; Mag leans against the wall after carrying in the food, watching the dancers swing and clasp their partners' hands. She can't help moving her feet to the music, and loses herself, longing to be taken up in it. Rubens, who has glanced over at her, almost loses his place; Moses, himself lost in the sounds his instrument is making, notices only the viola's gleaming mahogany and his bow above it. Raph, though, catches sight of her longing, and whispers to his partner before stepping out of his line and grabbing Mag by the waist.

She's worn her best party dress—a hand-me-down organdy print that Lucy has let out in the chest and down in the hem—and it fans out around her. Raph turns her in place by her good hand, tries to grab the other, but ends by laughing, holding her wrist, and whirling her out of the dance again. The music has stopped in this instant.

Angelica rises from the piano bench: 'Raph, no!" while Isba moves to Mag's side. "Are you hurt?" Mag shakes her head, trying to hide her distress, as the women of the household surround her and the dancers stand in shock and dismay.

"Did you see her *hand*?" one girl whispers to another.

Charles Willson strides forward, but Rubens has already taken his brother by the shirtfront; they are punching each other and rolling furiously on the dance floor as Rembrandt, yelling, tries to separate them and almost loses his balance in their thrashing. Their father, taking charge where he can, announces: "My friends, I apologize. This party is over."

The young girls titter and whisper in the hallway, their dresses fluttering; their brothers and potential beaus shake hands formally with Charles Willson and offer their regrets. It won't be the last time that he'll be embarrassed and disappointed by his oldest son. Older friends—Claypooles, Cadwalladers, Tilghmans, Moores—and Charles Willson's brother, James, linger with thanks and weather predictions before they leave, to let their host know, without saying so, that they understand and sympathize. "The girls play beautifully," Hannah, the Moores' grown daughter, remarks, suggesting that Raph's behavior doesn't reflect Charles Willson's abilities as a father. He presses her hand gratefully: "Thank you for saying so. They work very hard."

As she passes into her family's carriage in her gray silk dress, he wonders why he hasn't noticed her before: a graceful but modest woman with hazel eyes: A Quaker, not young but youthful, not beautiful but pleasing. "Sir," he says rashly—usually too proud to promote himself—hand on her father's arm, "if you'd like a family portrait, I'd be glad to oblige."

"A fine idea, sir," Mordecai Moore answers. "I'd thought of it, but hadn't arranged it." And Charles Willson will plan which paints can make a "speaking likeness" of Hannah, can capture the gold and green of her eyes. Painting her with her parents, he hopes to capture her stillness, her air of welcome, and would work slowly, to stay in her presence.

Chapter 24

"I WISH I COULD keep you here," Charles Willson says to Scar and Lucy when they've saved enough for a down payment on a house. "Especially you, Lucy; I'll miss your biscuits," he says jokingly, to hide a distress that can't help seeping through: "And I worry if you'll be all right."

Scar lifts their trunk into the trap Charles Willson has given them, along with the first horse Scar trained for him. "Sir, we're more than grateful," and shakes Charles Willson's hand, both men in outward agreement. Lucy, though, pulls Moses to her and bends over him, as if to take him back into her body. They both begin to cry, too hard to hear Scar: "You know it's for the best," and Mag standing by, offers: "It's not as if you'll be far away and you'll never see them, especially on your birthday."

Charles Willson, bound by law and unusually at a loss, tries to reassure: "Lucy, you know we'll take care of him. And yes, of course he can visit when you find a place."

The horse—well-trained as she is, but sensing the humans' distress—tosses her head, and Scar climbs into the trap. He reaches a hand to Lucy: "It's time," and she wrenches her body away from Moses and picks up her satchel. "I won't," she starts to say: *be the first to hear your voice crack, or see hair on your chin.* At Scar's cluck, the mare pulls them into the road to Philadelphia with a crunch of gravel. Dust billows behind them, hiding the carriage from Mag, Moses, and Charles Willson, who stand watching, until Mag takes Moses' hand and turns them back to the house. After he milks the cow next morning, Moses takes out his pocket knife and cuts a notch in the soft wood of the doorframe: one for each year before he turns twenty-six, before he can be free.

Mag wakes in the night, not sure what woke her; she hears the thrum of the grandfather clock's gears in the hall below, and then the soft percussion of worn metal on worn metal, striking three. The moon is a few days short of full, lopsided but strong enough to light the front drive and the path to the house. Full of clouds that stream in rows across it, the sky can't be called "mackerel": "furrowed" would describe it better, but she's never heard that term. The moon appears and disappears as the furrows cross it; she doesn't see the man in a long traveling coat approaching until he's right at the front door, which he tries to open with a rattling of the latch and barely-under-his-breath cursing. Raph. Who begins to shake and bang the resisting door, shouting, "Goddammit! Who locked it? It's never locked!"

"Fuck fuck fuck. . ." and a sound of kicking that Mag thinks must be loud enough to wake Charles Willson, who will—what? She runs to the front stairs and flies down them, barely feeling the treads under her feet. When she yanks the heavy door open, Raph bursts through on a wind of spirits and almost pushes her to the floor. Laughing, "You were waiting up for me!" he picks her up, unsteady as he is, and starts for the stairs. She inhales, under the whiskey smell, saddle soap and lavender, and instead of pulling away, puts her arms around the rough wool of his collar.

Struggling up the stairs, Raph, laughing and humming, lurching, almost dropping her, staggering upright—"You're heavier than I thought, bitch"—before he sees what Mag, face against his chest, cannot: Charles Willson in his nightshirt appearing out of the darkness above them.

"Good God, Raphaelle, what in Hell do you think you're doing? Let her go at once!"

"I thought you didn't believe in God or Hell, Charles Willson." Raph's speech is slower than normal but hasn't lost its edge, as he staggers up and his father takes a few steps down.

"Put her down, I said." Charles Willson's voice is low and menacing, as he takes a few more steps down.

"Oh, so you're sweet on her yourself? Isn't she a little young for you? And aren't you a little old? I'll bet you can't even. . . ."

At this, Charles Willson is close enough to grab Raph's arm, which causes his son to pull back and fall. He cries out in pain as his head strikes the edge of a step and he rolls with Mag into a heap. Charles Willson stands over them; in the faint moonlight spread across the floor, he looks like an avenging angel or an accusing ghost but sounds as stern and practical as Charles Willson:

"Mag, you need to be in bed. Are you hurt, or just drunk, Raph?"

He can't get back to sleep in the small room, more like a closet, where he's taken to sleeping apart from Eliza, saying he doesn't want to disturb her when he reads late, but really finds her tossing and unspoken complaints trouble *him*. Elbows on the sill, he watches the moon slide behind the western line of trees. *Has he done the right thing?* Always, if he looks hard enough, is Lydia, and the unanswerable questions: *Have I done enough to make it up to her? To atone?* Even though he doesn't call himself a Christian, this is the word that comes.

Tomorrow will be a long day with surveyors and the men who will build the dam he's designed; he can't afford a midday rest. He takes the bottle of clear liquid from the cabinet and measures a few drops of the laudanum into a glass; the water tastes slightly bitter, but he takes a long draught. When his brain finally stops churning, and his body sinks into the mattress, he sees the figure of a dark-skinned woman standing on a cliff, wind pushing her closer to the edge. Another figure runs toward her out of the darkness and tries with only one hand to pull her back: Mag, he realizes, and the other must be Lydia; their mouths are open but no screams come.

He startles awake, wondering if he himself has screamed, and if anyone has heard; only when the sky has begun to lighten does he fall asleep.

In the misty gray of dawn, light breaks over the far ridge through Mag's uncurtained window. She splashes more water onto her face than usual, as if the slight shock of it against her skin would clear the sleep from her eyes, her brain. Rubbing the washcloth hard against her forehead does nothing to erase the heaviness as she slips off her nightclothes and finds fresh drawers and a dress that was Angelica's: a bit too big, but clean.

Moses has built up the fire in the cookstove and gone for more wood; Peggy is bent to the coffee mill between her knees. She nods to Mag: "Water's on for the oats," which Mag lets fall like slow spring snow into the boiling pot.

She hears a groan, and turns; Raph is slumped on the wood box, his greatcoat half over his head. "Get the bootjack, girl." She kneels at his feet and pulls at the mud-caked heels, inhaling the rank smell as if it were incense and she were in the church of her childhood.

"Faster," Raph snarls and kicks a boot all the way off, throwing Mag off-balance. She's pushing herself off up the floor when Peggy notices: "Mag! The oatmeal!" and she turns to the stove just in time to save the heavy bubbling mass from sticking to the pot. Constant stirring with the longest wooden spoon is all that will do, and moving the pot from one burner to another, which requires two strong hands. Mag tries to budge it anyway, to drag it with what she has, when Moses slips his load of kindling into the firebox so quickly and quietly that she doesn't hear or see him until he's beside her. He doesn't speak as he pulls the pot to a cooler part of the stove. She barely nods her thanks, trying not to cry, and turns back to her stirring, even as the spoon stands up in the oatmeal, which threatens to turn to glue.

"Ugh," Isba passes by, on her way to the cupboard. "None of that for me." Raph brushes past, stumbling in his stockings, ordering, "Mag, bring my coffee to the dining room," but Peggy intercepts him: "You can get it yourself, Raph."

The voices, so alike in tone and timbre—father's and son's—rise and fall in volume but steady in intensity, go on for hours in the room below her. Mag listens with an ear to the floor, hearing only the anger: righteous and defensive; venomous and soothing; attacking and retreating. Someone would see if she crept closer; already too many in the household have noticed her attraction to Raph. Isba has begun to tease whenever she has an opportunity: "Mag's sweet on someone; guess who?" And Moses turns hopefully as Peggy shakes her head, *No*, and Mag turns away, blushing.

Raph leaves the next morning, his saddlebags packed full. He says goodbye to no one, waves to Mag without looking at her, and spurs his horse unnecessarily hard as they turn into the road. Peggy, looking for Mag to help turn the mangle, must lift her good hand finger by finger from the gate, and guide her back inside.

"But where will he go, Papa?" Angelica asks Charles Willson. "And how will he live?"

"Wherever he goes, he'll land on his feet," her father answers. It will be a year before a letter comes with a French stamp.

Chapter 25

IN STICK SEASON, Eliza is pregnant again and takes to her bed. Baby Titian takes his first steps, tugging at Angelica's skirts until she lifts him and offers a knob of bread dipped in honey. With the first snow, Mag imagines Raph's horse slipping, stumbling; when March turns to the heat of mid-June overnight, she wonders where he'll shed his heavy coat. Bread bowl between her knees, stirring flour and water together, she thinks in lines:

> *snow like sugar dusting your coat,*
> *but stinging, not sweet —*
> *i would be riding behind you*
> *to brush it off*

that make her feel there, as if her arms are around him: words that take the thought and make it something other than shapeless fear and longing. And she plans: After the bread is set in its bowl above the stove—kneaded and turned, her shovel hand the perfect implement—in the after-lunch lull she'll take down the notebook Charles Willson has let her keep on one of his library shelves, and write out the lines she's kept in her head, adding them to the others there: rough, not rhyming, saying nothing about God. No one knows that she does anything with her notebook but copy lines from books or practice her penmanship. If Charles Willson, reading and dozing in his afternoon haze, notices an intensity of attention in the way she bends to her page, he doesn't connect it to making art, which leaves her free, uninterrupted.

your hair is red in sunlight
as if fire has touched it —

if I
did
would it burn my hand?

Once she's written the words that have been in her head—and they're almost always about Raph—she doesn't feel she's brought him closer, but she's closer to herself: the one that no one knows, except sometimes Moses, and then when they were younger.

Loaves shaped and in the oven, she hears Argus' bark of alarm, horses' hooves and the rumble of wheels on gravel. Martha Ann Honeywell's brother, Josiah, jumps from their trap and holds the horse's bridle as his mother climbs down and approaches the front door Mag has opened to her anxious look before she can knock: "Is Mr. Peale here? It's the fever. . ."

"Do any of you have it?" Mag asks, alarmed in her turn, holding the door more than half-closed against her.

"No, no; we want to escape it. Is there any place out here where we can stay?"

Mag thinks of the playhouse Scar and Lucy have just left; she'd wanted to write in its quiet. "I'll find Mr. Peale," she says, ushering Mrs. Honeywell in.

Josiah carries his sister into the main house; Moses follows with their trunk on his back, watching Martha Ann's bright hair bounce on her brother's shoulder. Charles Willson is all benevolence: "Of course you are welcome here, dear Honeywells. How is it there?"

Peggy hurries to thin the soup for the extra guests, shaking her head while motioning to Mag to add places to the table. Mrs. Honeywell tells of bodies fallen in the street: "Their skin had turned yellow, and too many bodies for coffins to hold them were piled into a mass grave. People we know have died, but we had no way to mourn them. . ." She stops to draw a handkerchief from her bag.

Charles Willson steps forward to put his hand on her shoulder; his memories of Rachel's dying, of the fever that rises out of the swamps near the city, under the city, mix with his stronger sense of satisfaction at being someone's savior.

"I don't know how I can thank you, how I can repay you, sir." Mariah Honeywell says, but Charles Willson waves her concerns away with: "I hope you and your children will be comfortable enough here." He turns to Moses: "Go sweep the playhouse clean, and help the Honeywells with their bags. Mag, when you're done with the dishes, go help Moses."

Moses hasn't stopped looking at Martha Ann: her spindle legs, one with three toes wiggling off it; the empty sleeves of her fluttering blouse. Mag hides her irritation, lowering her head to gather up the plates. She's heard Moses, and even Charles Willson, talk about this miraculous artist with no hands, only a partial foot, and beautiful besides: the perfect museum attraction, and *sweetness itself.* Mag has been determined to hate her, but had never expected to meet her, let alone have to wait on her.

She has the broom, Moses the mop and pail. He's in a high good humor, as usual when he's away from the big house, and chatters on: "She cuts profiles with her teeth; you ought to see her, Mag. Maybe we can ask her to do one of us sometime," not noticing at first how furiously Mag is sweeping, releasing more dust into the room than she pushes into the dustpan close to his feet.

Thinking she's joking, he jumps over the broom and laughs, but she works as if punishing the floorboards, wanting to punish him.

"What's wrong?"

Mag throws down her broom. "I don't see why everybody thinks she's so wonderful, why we have to wait on her. . ." and she breaks into furious tears.

Moses takes the chance that she'll whirl on him, fist flailing, and puts his arm around her shuddering shoulders. "No one says how great *I* am," she says through sobs.

"But would you want them to?" They stand together as she quiets, takes up her broom and bends to the work. "Don't forget to mop around the hearth," she aims her words like arrows in his direction, before flinging herself out of the playhouse.

As if I'd forget! Moses thinks, but wisely doesn't say what he's thinking.

Peggy and Mag have cooked for three more and added places for the Honeywells at the dining table. "I miss Lucy every day," Peggy says, patching and folding the broken pie dough: "I can't remember what she did to keep this from happening. . . Damp weather must be coming."

Snapping the ends off the beans as fast as she can, Mag fears that if she says something, she'll let out more than she wants Peggy to hear.

"How do you think she eats?" Peggy asks the air. "The girl, I mean."

"Someone has to feed her." Moses has brought the lettuces to the sink.

Mag snorts in disgust: "Who would want to?"

Peggy starts to say, "Her mother takes such good care. . ." before Moses cuts in, "*I* would!" and Mag shakes the bowl of peas furiously at him, as if she'd throw it, and ends by pumping water as hard as she can into the sink.

Rubens rings the dinner bell, Josiah Honeywell carries his sister to the padded chair found for her, Peggy pushes Grandmother Peale in, Isba arrives in a flutter, Angelica carries baby Titian, Rembrandt strolls to his place. "Where's Charles Willson?"

In the sudden silence, the answer comes from the floor above: Eliza's voice rising in fury: "How could you? How could you bring these infected people into our home? And this *cripple*..." Words fail; she simply shrieks.

Charles Willson's low rumble follows, not reassuring, but righteously directive: "It's our duty to help others...."

"*All* others? Beggars off the street?'

"If you don't want to eat with them, Eliza, Mag can bring your dinner up here."

He excuses himself to the company, taking his place in front of the Sunday roast, sharpening his carving knife with a flourish. Mrs. Honeywell hardly misses a beat: "It's lovely to be here, Charles Willson. I'm Mariah Honeywell," she nods to the group from her place next to her daughter, who opens her small mouth—like a baby bird, Mag thinks—for a spoonful of soup. Moses, in his swift, graceful way, is at their side before anyone has noticed him moving. "I can do that, ma'am, if you want to eat your own meal."

No one notices that Mag has taken her plate to the kitchen, where she eats with a book held open by her plate. "Charles Willson will kill you if you spill any food on his book," Moses brushes past her with a stack of dishes to be washed. She doesn't look at him: "He gave me this; it's mine." Keats: an extra copy just come from friends in London. She wants to keep it with her, propped against the sink, but tries to see how far her memory will reach:

When I have fears that I may cease
to be

and can't get further. At their lessons, assigning poems to learn by heart, James has said: "Memory takes practice and gives rewards. If you have a poem in your head, you can always turn to it when you have nothing to read."

Dishes dried and gleaming—she and Moses have always worked well together, flourishing the dish-towels, almost dancing, never breaking a plate or glass, but this day she snatches the heavy platter from him and almost falls trying to hold onto it.

"Mag, I was just trying to help."

She fails to hide anything from Moses: "You talk about her all the time, how she cuts profiles, how pretty she is!" She throws the damp towel at his feet.

"Why do you care?" he asks, angry in his turn, as she flounces away with her book.

Martha Ann has a low speaking voice, full of melody, and when the Peales gather with their instruments in the drawing room after dinner, Angelica asks her: "Would you like to sing, Martha Ann?"

"I would. But please let me be just *Martha.*"

At first, the three women make a trio, singing part of a Purcell opera a friend has sent Charles Willson. Although she tries not to outshine the others, Martha's clear alto can't be hidden. The Peale sisters step back and let her continue. "You have to be Dido," Isba says, handing her the lead part.

Mag, whose singing voice doesn't match her love of music, and who hides, mouthing the words, in the chorus, thinks sourly: *Of course she has a beautiful voice!* If anyone suggested that she was jealous, she would have been astounded, then outraged: *Jealous? She can do hardly anything by herself . . .* And would have been even more outraged if anyone dared suggest that what upsets her most is Moses' attraction: *He just feels sorry for her,* she'd say, if given a chance.

For his part, Moses is in awe of Martha—her grace and inge-
nuity—but has no one with whom to share his enthusiasm. He
knows Mag well enough to hide his joy when Martha praises his
skill at feeding her: cutting her meat into the exact right sizes for
her small mouth; timing each new mouthful to her readiness to
receive it.

"You're a genius!" she exclaims, and he ducks his head to hide
his pleasure. She becomes almost his religion: an emotion so pure
and lacking in self-interest, it raises her far above him. If Mag has
been his comrade, his equal, true friend, Martha is his goddess,
and Mag is lost.

She hasn't found her way to her notebook and pen for days since
the Honeywells arrived, with more meals to cook and clean up
from, more bedclothes to change. A current of discontent troubles every interaction; Eliza's complaints spill from her bedroom
despite its closed door. She petitions everyone who'll listen, even
Angelica and Isba, who don't pretend to be polite. Mag, though,
is pinned to the doorframe, unable to disagree when Eliza hurls
out her bile: "You can't like them either; there's a lot more work
for you—and to have to look at that freak eating . . ." She makes
a sound of disgust, raising herself up from her pillows with such
urgency that Mag fears she may vomit the breakfast she's just
eaten.

Then, helpless, Eliza falls back against the pillows, waving Mag away: "Go . . . go . . . bring ice water." But she can't,
even in her weakness, refrain from adding: "Oh, ask Peggy; you
would drop it."

Downstairs, Charles Willson is pulling on his gloves; he hasn't
been to the city since the fever was reported, and now ignores
Mrs. Honeywell's: "Do be careful, Charles Willson; there's fever
even in the center of town."

He tugs at the bandana he's tied around his neck and pulls it playfully over his nose, winking: "Dear lady, of course I'll take care!" A little current of flirtation is running between them: something to leaven the dullness of their so similar days and the protests from upstairs. Mariah Honeywell isn't young, but she's not too old to be flattered by Charles Willson's attention; she preens a bit and smooths her shirtwaist over her breasts. "We'll be picking the last of the ramps today," she offers, knowing the treat will please him and showing that she's joined the household.

He's gone with another flick of his bandana, and gives his horse her head. He spends the day in the almost deserted city, sweeping the Long Room, dusting the glass fronts of its displays; light fills the space, even though it's a cloudy day. He doesn't visit Gloriana until evening, once her busiest time, but quiet now, with the fever abroad. One of her girls takes his dusty coat; another pulls off his mud-spattered boots. "Bring a basin with warm water and lavender, love," Gloriana's commands are gentle but meant to be instantly obeyed. Charles Willson's feet luxuriate in warmth and delicate scent; he can't remember ever being so well treated.

"What will you have?" The woman opposite him asks, and when food and drink are ordered, "What brings you in this dangerous time?"

"Home is more dangerous to me,' he says bluntly. "She makes me so angry I could kill her," not needing to explain to Gloriana which *she* he means. "I want to throw something at her, break something. I'm afraid I can't keep from hurting her."

"It's worse all of a sudden?'

"She's pregnant again," he answers, not looking at her.

"So soon?" Gloriana asks mildly, and takes a sip of her whiskey: nonchalant, as if to remove the tinge of judgment.

"I'd had too much to drink, and had no other way to stop her whining: *You don't love me. . . . if you really loved me, you'd. . . . "* and he shakes his head.

"Charles Willson," Gloriana sits straight in her chair and takes a different tone: "you've invented so much"—she takes note of his blush of pleasure and takes a tack he doesn't expect—"like all the teeth you've made"—here she shows his handiwork in her smile—"why can't you find some way to keep your wives from getting pregnant?"

He flinches, as if she's struck him, and tenses, searching for a reply.

"Short of just staying away from them or pulling out in time, I mean. I thought you were acquainted with Mrs. Brigham when you were in London. She sells these at a good price." She pulls a pale pink scrap from her dressing-table drawer and twirls it on two fingers: "Like this? Just a bit of pig intestine. . ."

His face reddens; he can't meet her eyes, which makes her explode with laughter: "Charles Willson, I thought nothing could embarrass you! I thought you knew all the beddable women on two continents. . ."

He struggles to explain: "I thought they were just to prevent disease . . . if you thought you might catch it from someone. . ."

She takes pity on his discomfort: "All my girls ask their clients to use them; any man who refuses has to see me. Yes, they prevent the clap, but also unwanted pregnancy."

"You never asked. . ." he begins.

"You don't know what I have up my sleeve, as it were. One child to support is enough for me." She puts a stiff circle of the same pale pink stuff up to her eye like a monocle. She turns aside and takes a long draught of her whiskey.

Bent almost double, as if to make himself smaller, elbows on his knees, he raises his head: "A daughter?"

"Living with her grandmother, where no one knows what her mother does."

"And her father?"

Gloriana takes another draught of whiskey. "Are you staying the night?"

"If I may," he answers. Then, "Do you have a portrait of her?" And to her silence: "Would you like one?"

"If I could afford it." Flatly, as if not taking him into account, with the lack of guile or coy suggestion that makes men trust her, makes some think they're in love.

He answers by crossing the room to her: "I think I could arrange it," but is interrupted by the double knock on the door that signals an emergency. everyone in the house knows not to interrupt Gloriana when she's with someone unless it's absolutely necessary.

"Excuse me," she says to Charles Willson, and steps into the hall, half-closing the door behind her. He can hear a hasty exchange of lowered voices before she turns back to him. "I must go"—which means he must, too. "Another girl on the run, and we must hide her where no one will look. Do you think that patrol has gone back where they came from?"

"I can find out. . . ." Charles Willson hesitates in helplessness.

"What we'll do must be done right away." She holds the door open for his exit.

Chapter 26

WAKING TO A RUSH OF WIND catching her bedroom shutter, Mag's heart leaps at the sound. Clouds are flying past the almost-full moon, one minute hiding, the next revealing no winded horse, no weary rider: only the empty yard in its cold silver light.

If you come for me—
whenever you come —
you part the dark

She hears the lines, hopes she can hold onto them until she can find her pen and notebook, and the time to fasten them to paper.

If the wind that shakes the tree,
strong wind that wakes me,
could blow you this way,
blow you to me —

She'll try to keep the words in her mind until she wakes again, hold them through the morning's chores, the *Mind the oatmeal*

don't stick now; Can you help me with this, Mag? Charles Willson
needs you to clean his brushes, brush his coat. Lettuces need washing;
Pigs need slopping. . .

In the blessed after-lunch lull, she opens the library door gin-
gerly, to find Charles Willson sound asleep, without the usual
book open on his stomach and glasses askew on his forehead.
When did he get in? Holding her breath, she retrieves her pen
and notebook from the shelf where she'd left them, and begins.

What happens when she looks back—looks into the night
when wind swept the shutters to trembling, the three-quarter
moon lit the yard and the road beyond, in spite of the cloud
covering it—the words come differently, come stronger, as if she
didn't know what she felt before, so overcome by seeing it:

> *O wind that sweeps the road,*
> *so strong you overturn the stones,*
> *if you could carry him to me,*
> *you could lift me, dash me down,*
> *do what you want —*

What happens then is that her pen trembles in her hand as
she pushes it hard to the page and finds this isn't quite what she
wanted, or not quite enough:

> *If you come on the wind,*
> *so strong it can lift your horse,*
> *I'll wait at the open door —*
> *open open for you —*
> *even if that's not what you want*

And then she wants to say something harder, closer to true:

> *Catch me up against your coat*

again, your cheek burning mine,
lay me down after your journey,
I won't be afraid this time —

and is living in her poem, when Charles Willson gives such a groan that she jumps, having forgotten he's there. "Mag, come pull my boots off." He's fallen asleep with them on. "And bring coffee like a good girl."

She blushes as if he's seen into the notebook she pushes back on the shelf, behind the books. "What've you been reading, Mag?"

"Oh, this and that, sir," she calls over her shoulder, knowing he's only remembering to be *Charles Willson, kind master*, and won't remember her answer.

His boots are so caked with mud, and his feet have swelled so overnight, that she'd need two strong hands to do the job, and even then, they might not be enough. "I'll have to get the jack, sir." She almost cries with frustration and the shame of not doing what's expected of her.

"Oh, get Moses or Rube," he commands airily, not seeing her distress and not, as he inhales his coffee, realizing she's disobeyed, coming back with the bootjack and placing one mud-covered boot in it. Seeing a small sign of progress as the heel fits the wooden curve, she urges him, "You have to help, sir," taking pleasure in telling him what to do.

Feet free, he sighs with relief. "What would I do without you, girl? Don't bother with these stinking socks; I'll wash them myself." Mag rocks back on her heels, relieved in her turn, until his next request, "But please get the mud off the boots; I have to go out again tonight."

"But sir," she begins, "Peggy says Eliza. . ." and as if on cue, a scream comes from upstairs, angry as much as afraid.

The labor is long and hard; Antigua has been called. Eliza is in so much distress that she can't complain about the color of Antigua's skin and accepts the cool cloths on her forehead and the hand that holds hers as she arches against the bed. Hours go by with no sign of change. Moses runs for the doctor, who shakes his head, calls for a basin of boiled water for his instruments, and clean towels and sheets: anything to stanch the blood. And a glass of whiskey that Antigua holds to Eliza's parched lips.

The doctor hates having to cut the distended belly, pushing aside the layers of fat to reach the pulsing womb, and fearing his knife will cut too deep. But there is the round head, easy to pull up and out, while the feet dangle close to the cervix: another son. "Another contrarian, Charles Willson, wanting to come out feet first," he tells the father, accepting a glass and raising it to the newest Peale.

He will be named Benjamin Franklin, after the friend who, whenever he visits, advises the children, including—and perhaps particularly—Mag: *Persevere*, in concern for this child, who cries without ceasing until a wet nurse can be found.

Eliza may not even have seen him as he was lifted out of her body; she drifts in and out of consciousness all the first day and night.

Mag, bringing a cup of broth on the chance that Eliza will raise her head, steps back to avoid the river of red that flows under the bedroom door. "Peggy!" she screams, but the sheets and towels they bring won't sop it all up, won't stop its flow. Eliza's face turns blue, then gray; Charles Willson sits by her head, holding her hand as it cools in his palm. Franklin, as he'll be called, thrives; his grandparents, Eliza's parents, refuse to speak to Charles Willson.

The funeral is a small, ragged parade to the family graveyard, with mourners who aren't mourning a woman they never loved. Charles Willson struggles to find proper words: *We are as dust, and to dust we will return.* He wipes his sweaty forehead often, although the day is cool and windy. A few neighbors have come: the Randolphs—Jeff ostentatiously blowing his nose; Arabella sincerely weeping. If Eliza was close to anyone, it was Arabella, who gossiped with her in a sisterly way, complained about "the help," and sympathized with her anger when Charles Willson manumitted Scar and Lucy—without of course admitting it was she who called out the Slave Patrol.

Scar and Lucy have arrived on a single horse, Lucy riding behind Scar with her arms around his waist and her head on his shoulder. She runs to Moses and holds him in a long clasp, once or twice stepping back to hold his face in her hands and look, as if memorizing him. Scar strides to Charles Willson, who greets him, hand outstretched: "Scar, thank you for coming."

"It's *Thomas* now, sir: *Thomas Williams*. Lucy is still *Lucy;* she was so well-known for baking, but she's *Williams* too, not *Peale.*"

Charles Willson, shaking Thomas' hand, looks down to hide his hurt—irrationally, he knows—and comes back to the self he likes to be: "How are you both? You look well."

"Business is good, thanks to you for sending so much our way. We wanted to bring you our condolences"—and here again the other man can't meet his gaze; he doesn't need sympathy for a loss he doesn't feel. "And we wanted to see our boy. Is he doing well?"

On firmer ground, Charles Willson can show his usual enthusiasm: "Moses is the best profile cutter I've ever seen: faster and more accurate than I or any of my boys. Or even Martha Ann," he adds, sensing Mariah Honeywell nearby.

"And he gives you no trouble?" Thomas asks, almost as if he wishes to hear the opposite, as if hoping some reason could be found to release his son.

Peggy is beside them, wiping her hand on her apron before extending it: "I couldn't do without him, but we miss you."

"Especially Lucy?" Thomas raises his eyebrows as his wife joins him. Without hesitation, she and Peggy embrace. "Oh Lucy, I wish you'd been here these past few days, getting this meal ready. Charles Willson wants everything just right, even though. . . ."

Lucy doesn't need to be told the reason. "Anything I can do now?"

Angelica, Isba, and Mag crowd around them, eager for direction, for the kitchen to hum again. Lucy bends to look more carefully at Mag: "And how are you, girl?"

"I miss you," Mag answers, and Lucy finds in her face and in her voice more missing than she'll say.

"You've grown up, Mag," Lucy finds the right words, "just in the few months I've been away." She puts both her hands on Mag's shoulders and holds her at arms' length: "I almost forgot how pretty you are."

Mag flushes with pleasure and then flushes deeper with delight and the fear of having that delight exposed, as hoofbeats pound in off the Philadelphia Road and Raph—hair flying, coat flapping, bandana over his nose like a highwayman—pulls up in the yard.

"Scar!" he shouts, running to embrace him, before shaking his father's hand, moving swiftly to evade questions; kissing each of his sisters, Peggy, and Lucy, before hesitating in front of Mag. He leans to graze her cheek with his, as Rubens calls from the wagon where they've loaded the coffin: "About time you got here, Raph. We need you to dig."

It's a rough affair—the wagon lurching, the wooden box slipping over the stony farm track to the graveyard—but they lay poor Eliza to rest. The girls have picked daffodils and strewn them across the red earth.

The food is as abundant as Charles Willson has wanted and satisfies the hunger that follows a funeral: that primal need to be restored. It isn't as elegant—as Arabella whispers to a neighbor behind her fan—as it would have been with Lucy in the kitchen, but it serves: the ham and biscuits, creamed oysters and vinegar-laced greens. A three-layer frosted cake that Mag has made with Peggy's help separating the eggs. Ice cream that Rubens churns, golden on the blades. And drink: every male neighbor has brought a bottle that they empty as night comes on and the women and girls are sent home.

Mag, though, is still on her feet after eighteen hours, bringing pitchers of ice water to the men in the drawing room, taking the empty bottles away.

"Mag, come give us a song!" Raph yells in her direction. Has she ever confessed to him her fear of singing? It seems as if he sees her shame, no matter how she tries to hide it. Her voice is strangled when she answers: "Try Angelica or Isba, or," with sudden inspiration, "ask Martha," which creates a sudden silence that Raph fills, pounding out a marching song on the harpsichord.

Charles Willson is on his feet, gesturing to Mag to leave the room, sweeping Raph's glass of whiskey to the floor. "I'll ask you to leave, my friends," and they do, stumbling, crowding one another in their haste to get through the door. Other evenings with Raph have ended this way, and other evenings with their own sons: their farewells are inflected with fellowship.

Chapter 27

IN THE GRAY MORNING—always a gray morning after a sleep-less night—Moses holds his bowl of coffee and hot milk against his chin, the steam washing his face. "It should have been raining," he says. Peggy frowns, pauses in her kneading, and is about to speak, when Mag says "It was too beautiful a day." Without having to ask, she knows what Moses means, just as, when they were younger, each would finish the other's sentences. She pulls back from this rush of kinship: "Aren't you feeding your girlfriend this morning?"

"She's still asleep," he answers mildly, not bothering to antag-onize her, as he usually does when she baits him: *She's not my girlfriend,* but blushing, she can tell.

As if he's heard her meanness and is embarrassing her, Raph rushes in—he's always rushing, always in transit. "Peggy, my love, is breakfast ready?" And takes only a cold bun from the day before, and a long draught of coffee.

"If you can wait a minute, young sir, fresh rolls will be ready," Peggy tries to leaven her annoyance with the playful address. She never uses *sir* for anyone, even Charles Willson. "Mag can get you a flask to take that coffee with you."

Mag wants to protest, *My hands are shaking too much*, but does as she's bidden, head bent to her task of not spilling a drop, not noticing that Moses is watching.

"Hurry up, will you? I have someone waiting in the city," Raph urges, but the three in the kitchen suspect he's hurrying to evade Charles Willson, who came close to knocking him unconscious the night before.

Mag lifts the heavy silver pot, thankful for the olive-wood handle, but in her nervousness misses the rim of the cup, which trembles in its saucer. She runs for a rag to mop the spill, but Raph intercepts her: "Oh, don't bother; I'll just take a sip and go," and almost collides with Charles Willson coming in the kitchen door as he is going out. Neither acknowledges the other.

With a clatter of hooves and creaks of leather, Raph is gone, back down the Germantown Road, greatcoat and hair flying behind him.

When will I see you
Will I ever see you
Will you ever see me

The words come, and she despairs of holding onto them, as Charles Willson asks her to sweep up last night's broken glass in the drawing room, and Moses is beside her, with the dustpan. Does she thank him? She's too preoccupied to notice he's there.

Rubens flings a bunch of mud-caked carrots onto the kitchen table; clods fly across the scrubbed surface and roll to the floor. "Rube!" Peggy turns to stop him, but he's gone again without a word. In the past few months, he's hardly spoken at meals, and brings in the vegetables in with only a curt "Here's what you asked for," without the usual pride in describing each crop. Peggy thinks to have a word with Charles Willson, but he's gone again to the city, as he is almost every day now, often taking Moses with him.

At dinner that night, when Rubens finishes his third glass of wine, has eaten with his head down, and barely spoken to anyone beyond, *Please pass the butter,* Charles Willson pushes his plate aside and looks intently at this son, who works hard without complaint, showing a shy pride in the plants he grows and brings to the table a quiet presence beside his more assertive brothers.

"How is the garden this year? Do you need more seeds, tools?"

"I need help," Rubens answers flatly, looking hard at his father.

"We can't afford to hire more men. There's the dam to build; I just put out the word." The dam is Charles Willson's new pet project: damming the river where it flows past his fields, building a mill to run on its force. He's been describing it to Thomas Jefferson, complaining of the cost of hired labor to realize his plans, to which Jefferson is sympathetic but can offer no solution. His own help he can't recommend to his abolitionist friend, his own imagination limited only by the endurance and skill of the bodies he controls and the money he can borrow.

"This farm needs vegetables more than a dam." Rubens speaks with the weight of all he's drunk.

Charles Willson considers how little he knows this quiet boy, now a young man, and how easily he has dismissed him as a lesser artist. "I may have to sell." For the first time, he puts into words the thought that's been disturbing his sleep.

Which rouses Rubens: "And do what?"

"Go back to my pencil. And run the museum." Which he's been collecting for, rented the rooms for, half-run for years now. As soon as the words are out of his mouth, they announce a new reality: a plan: "Would you like to help run it, Rube?"

The son knows he hasn't a choice, unless, like Raph, he runs away. The absurdity of his father's question strikes him, and he laughs—the irony of which escapes his father, who thinks his son has had a change of heart, of mood, and reaches to take his hand in a congratulatory shake. "There's a lot of work to do." Charles Willson's preferred mode: industry driving out regret and despair.

Next, he must persuade Mariah Honeywell that it's safe to return to the city; every day when he comes back from a day of oiling the museum's floors and adding to exhibits, he pulls off the bandana covering his nose and announces: "Fewer deaths today."

"Reported," she answers, but when he offers Martha Ann a new place to receive her profile customers—a regal chair by a tall window in the Long Room, where sunlight will fall on her for most of the day, turning her blond hair to spun gold—Mariah begins to relent and pack their things.

With Charles Willson taking Moses to the city, and Josiah Honeywell gone to ready his family's house for their return, Martha's feeding falls to Mag, who brings a tray with soup, bread, lettuce: just enough to carry safely. "I'll go back for the cider," she says without looking at Martha, who is bent over a paper spread out below the pen in her mouth, her feet holding scraps of colored fabric.

"I'd rather have water, please." The other young woman speaks around her pen.

"Are you ready to eat now?" Mag asks, noticing the scraps, their colors and shapes, and the scissors. "Or would you like me to come back later?" The last thing she wants to do is feed this young woman so close to her age and dangerously like her: to hold a spoon to her lips and be patient enough to wait while she sips, chews, swallows. She would hate to *be* her, as much as she hates the admiration others give her.

When she comes back with the glass of water, carrying it carefully with her good hand and her partial one for support, she looks for a place to set it where she won't knock it over onto the scraps on the work table. "What're you working on?"

"The Lord's Prayer. There will be fur and tree-tips and leaves and flowers, with the words in the middle."

Mag doesn't ask how paper can be fur; as she looks at the rectangle, she sees that Martha has colored it tan and rose, decorated it with branches and blossoms and fringed the edges.

Martha's mouth has been writing "Our Father Who Art in Heaven" across a circle of white paper in a tiny, clear script. She drops her pen in her lap, lets it roll onto the table where she can reach it again. "I'm hungry."

Mag adjusts a large napkin across Martha's chest and lap and dips her spoon into the bright green soup—watercress today—and tries to hold her hand steady at Martha's lips; the spoon knocks against teeth too many times and is sometimes too full. Martha sputters and spits out some.

"I'm sorry; I'm not good at this."

"Moses is better," Martha says shortly.

"It must be hard to have someone else do this for you," Mag ventures.

"Not as bad as having your mother wipe your bum. You can't know. . ."

But Mag takes offense: "I can imagine."

Then, sensing they're at a stalemate, and knowing it's ridiculous to defend her own powers of imagination, Mag scrambles to turn the conversation: "But couldn't you feed yourself?"

"How can you tell me what I can do?"

"I mean, if the food is at the right height for you to reach it, if the soup was in a cup you could drink from, if the meat was cut in small pieces, and the bread torn. . ."

"And my feet can hold a plate as well as this paper." She bends double to the tray Mag brings with adjustments and looks up at her with green lips: "Yes."

When her mother looks in: "Where's the girl? I thought she was helping you. . ." she sees Martha taking her food with her mouth and legs, and hides her disappointment: "How wonderful! You figured how to do this on your own!" It's one more way that her daughter will leave her.

"That does look like fur!" Mag exclaims of the rose-colored cutout flocked with feathery tracings and fringed along the edges. She can't help exclaiming, although, when Martha is working, she tries not to interrupt her, noticing that she must drop one handle of her scissors to her lap before she speaks.

Now Martha laughs: "Yes! It's just paper, but I drew on it and drew on it." She nudges the shapes with her toes: "I want to have fur, leaves and flowers, all showing the glory of God."

Mag doesn't know what to say when Martha talks about God; how can she be sure there is one? In the Peale house, what gods there are are work and reason.

Martha moves the scraps into place on the work table: "This is how they'll look when I'm done." The furry piece goes first, and on it the circle with the prayer written inside a ring of leaves, circled by roses, bounded by more and smaller leaves.

"Will you sign your name on it?"

"No, I just want to say how I made it. I'm not sure where the words should go."

"Maybe in the circle, after the other writing?"

"I'm not sure I can fit it in—but yes, it was God writing through me." She bends with the pen in her teeth, drops it, and pulls back: "There's no room."

"Do you want me to try?" Mag ventures.

"You want it to say. . .?"

"Written without hands."

The finished work will read in tiny capital letters, "WRITTEN WITHOUT HANDS," in Mag's handwriting, below "The Lord's Prayer" written in tiny script by Martha's pen.

"It needs more color," Martha leans back and squints. "Pine tips in the corners, I think." Her toes select a green scrap from the pile in front of her, folds it double, and begins to cut. Mag is spellbound as a small branch separates from its surround, fringed on the edges and lacy at the center. Martha's mouth and toes work each end of the scissors; her face flushes and sweats. When the scissors drop, she raises her head, "Thank you for not saying anything."

"What would I say?"

"The people who come to the museum to watch me cut profiles always whisper to each other, and then one will come closer to ask: 'How do you do that?' I can't answer with the scissors' end in my mouth, so one always says: 'Can she talk?' Usually I keep cutting, but sometimes I let the scissors fall and say: 'The Lord helps me.' That keeps them quiet."

"Do you believe that, about the Lord?"

"I do. I call on Him the whole time I'm cutting: *I will lift mine eyes unto the hills:* that one; do you know it?" But Mag shakes her head. "I keep praying, so I don't even know they're watching. . . . Does anyone ask what happened to your hand?"

"They did before I came here, but now no one pays much attention. Or if they do, Charles Willson frowns at them. You know how he frowns?"

Martha laughs: a surprising, and surprised, sound, as if she herself didn't know she could make it.

"Charlie would pester me and pester me when he first came. I'd just say, 'It's always been this way,' over and over, until one day Moses got mad, 'She told you and told you,' and punched him."

"Punched? Moses?"

"In the stomach, just hard enough to knock the breath out of him."

"Moses likes you," Martha says.

"He likes you best. He thinks you're an angel."

Martha shakes her head, and her whole body with it: "I'm not, and it's wrong to think so."

"He wants to marry you, I bet, when he grows up."
"Has he ever said so? I need white, I need money."

Anyone looking at them, as Peggy does, looking for Mag, would
see two young women sharing a confidence, Martha's delivered
with thrilling bluntness; would see beauty in the head of brown
hair that turns red in sunlight, in the blonde curls that seem like
spun gold; in the flash of brown eyes and deep blue ones; in a high
cheekbone and the lift of a chin. Peggy, about to ask Mag to help
her change sheets, steps back out of the doorway, but not quite
out of earshot.

"Any prospects?" Mag asks, newly confident of a frank answer.

Martha gives the smile of someone holding onto a secret.
"Some." And seems to leave it there, but is only pausing to consider. "You'll find some men who're just curious, want to see if you
have breasts and a slot like anyone else."

Mag's eyes open wider; she's on the brink of a cliff, exhilarated
and terrified, ready to follow wherever Martha leads.

"You can tell those right away, and then there are others who
think you're not human, more like a saint."

"Like Moses?"

"Like Mo." She uses a nickname that Mag has never heard
anyone else use, or thought of herself: familiar. "You just have
to use some swear words to shock them, or be mean to them, to
scare them, make them go away. It's the ones you fall in love with
that you have to look out for."

"What are they like?"

"Good-looking, fast-moving. Like Raph."

Mag flushes painfully, and lowers her head, hoping Martha
hasn't noticed.

"What you want, what I want, is someone with that flash, that
spirit, but kind. Your Raph would never make you anything but
miserable. I pity the woman who marries him."

"I never. . ." Mag starts to say, but Martha cuts her off: "I see how you look at him. He sees it too. He laughs at you."

"He does?" Mag is so innocent, so ripe for ruin, that Martha is almost irritated. Was she ever so defenseless?

"Mag, he'd love to break you. Don't let him into this house, put him out of your mind."

Mag pushes the forgotten tray of food closer. "Is there anything I can get you? I should go." She can't bear to hear more.

Martha smiles, the superior smile of knowing more than Mag: "*I* don't need anything. *You* need to forget him."

And Mag is gone.

Every evening when Charles Willson comes back from the city, Mariah Honeywell pesters: "How many funerals did you see? How many people are sick?"

He throws off his coat as he'd like to throw off her questions: "It seems to be getting better," and moves to the kitchen: "How are you girls faring? When's dinner? How's the vegetable crew without Rube?"

Peggy, annoyed to be one of the "girls," snaps: "Dinner's almost ready. By the time you wash and go through your mail, it'll be on the table."

"And the new vegetable crew?" He means Isba and Charlie, who have taken Rubens' place in the garden, along with the younger ones: Linnaeus and Franklin, who aren't much help. The boys argue over which row is whose to weed, which green sprout is edible, which a weed; when a pea pod is fat and ready to be picked, and Franklin eats most of what he picks. Angelica, who would have been the best judge, is mostly indoors, trying to find order in Charles Willson's untidy accounts, as the household shifts its tasks, its balance, contracts and expands in different directions.

With Eliza's death, Charles Willson seems set adrift: relieved of a burden, exhilarated and searching. He has thrown himself into building the museum: a project he can complete with less help than anything on the farm, which now confounds him. The mill he envisions will require workers who'd need to be paid, and he'd need to supervise them.

Will he sell? The question, once released into air, lingers without a definite answer, acts like a river diverted from its course, flowing through the house. A current that can be seen in Rembrandt's silences, his plans to go abroad that never materialize; in Peggy's irritation; Mag's sudden tears; the girls' quarrels; the boys' ceaseless squabbling. No one, in fact, sleeps well. Once Mag, going down the stairs in search of a glass of milk, bumps into Charles Willson coming up at three in the morning. He reads late and later, unable to face the frustration of trying and failing to sleep, and ashamed of reaching for the laudanum bottle.

Meals have become a study in distraction: children running to the kitchen for something extra or forgotten; Grandmother Peale demanding more cake, forgetting she's just had a piece; Mariah Honeywell's unanswerable questions about the end of the fever. Franklin refuses to eat altogether, no matter what Peggy tries to give him. She asks Moses to see if Anna, skilled at taking care of children, might come to help.

No one asks permission of Charles Willson or the Randolphs, and no one makes a plan. It's simply understood that Anna will slip away into this other household, and that another house slave— probably her sister, Aurelia, will take her place. The Randolphs are unlikely to notice; Arabella prides herself on not being able to tell one Black face from another, and Jeff cares more about his next drink than his estate's management, as long as his crops are growing and getting to market.

So Anna slips into the kitchen to make simple meals, rocking her own Elijah in a cradle on the floor with her free hand. Peggy will cook extra for her, and makes a pallet soft with quilts in the attic room that Scar and Lucy used when they first came. When Anna offers to help with cooking and cleaning, Peggy waves her away: "You have enough to do. Mag helps me just fine."

Mag, overhearing, feels complimented, but still wishes Peggy had accepted the offer. She notices a tenderness between them— blunt Peggy, gentle Anna—the affinity that grows between women working toward a common goal: unspoken understandings, and even—in the lingering hand Mag notices on Anna's shoulder— the affection of a mother for a child, a sister for a sister, a lover for a lover. Affections Mag senses without having felt them.

Charles Willson, coming into the kitchen, is surprised to see Anna. Unlike many white men, he does notice Black faces, but says nothing. The kitchen is Peggy's domain, and when she draws him aside to explain, he nods his assent, indicating the sleeping Franklin: "Good idea, my friend. The proof's right here."

One morning after the laudanum has failed to soothe his seething brain and he's paced, paced from one end of the house to the other, window to window, longing for dawn, he's startled by Yarrow Mahmout, coming in with a basket of bristling greens: "Antigua sent you some chamomile, sir, and some St. John's Wort for your nerves."

"Oh, how did you know I need something?" But Yarrow just smiles and puts the bunches of herbs in the sink. "I'll make you a tea and show Peggy or Mag how to serve it."

"Stay with me a while, will you?" Charles Willson surprises himself by the naked need of his question, and covers it with heartiness: "There're biscuits cooking, and coffee on. Please sit."

As they eat together, the household moving around them at its chores, Charles Willson watches the other man's face, wanting to prolong the calm that's come over him. "Yarrow, my man, can I paint you?"

"Well, sir, of course, any color you want, but I can't pay you."

"As payment for the medicines you've brought. And I'll paint you the color you are. I'm not sure I have everything I need in my painting room here, but we can begin. If you don't mind sitting here for a while."

During this time, they talk: of Yarrow's journey from Africa, his years enslaved; his work when free; the house he bought, and sold to buy the farm he has now. Charles Willson knows how to catch his subject's face in repose so quickly that conversation won't interrupt a stilled expression. So they make the portrait that will hang in the Long Room's Gallery of Notables, without Eliza, Charles Willson thinks in guilty relief, to complain that he's wasting his time. All of his skill goes into making Yarrow's skin tone as warm as his expression; although Yarrow isn't smiling, he looks at the painter as if opening his soul.

After Yarrow has pronounced, "It is Yarrow himself," the painting is done, and the household settles a little, although Charles Willson's rootlessness still infects it. He's gone to the city almost every day now, taking Rubens and often Moses with him. The force of his interest moves away from the farm, even as he works to maintain it. Ever needing to plan, he begins to look for a wife, asking his friends if they know *any nice single women.* Ever cautious, and easily embarrassed, he also tells those friends: "Don't let anyone else know I'm looking."

He's unable to speak with the very young women who come with their parents to sit for their portraits; he doesn't know what pleases them, has never heard of the novels they talk of reading as they fan their faces and try to sit as still as possible.

He finds himself snapping too often in irritation: "Miss, please hold your pose."

And they jump and adjust themselves in their light flowered silks, thinking how grouchy and old this famous Mr. Peale is.

Then one day Mordecai Moore, the Quaker banker, and his wife, Elizabeth, come with their daughter Hannah, not to have a family portrait done, but to have their profiles cut. Charles

Willson, a bit disappointed, and busy arranging cabinets in the Long Room, recommends Moses. "I'd rather have you, sir," Moore says, surprising Charles Willson, who thought Quakers more open-minded.

Hannah Moore, though, steps forward: "I'll have the boy do mine." She's tall and brown-haired, dressed in grays and browns: not young but smooth-skinned and alert. She sits with such ease before Moses with his scissors that Charles Willson, looking in, is arrested by her calm—and Moses' as he works. The sun that falls into the room has picked up strands of red, gold, and gray in the hair edging her bonnet, and the gold-and-green in the brown of her eyes.

"Pardon me, Miss," he ventures, "would you sit for a portrait?"

"Oh, but I couldn't afford your prices, sir," she answers, with Quaker simplicity and not a trace of the coquetry he finds in more fashionable women.

"It would be my pleasure to paint you," he blurts, then catches himself as if he's suggested something unseemly. "I mean, I would do it for nothing but the privilege."

She smiles slightly, with the unruffled calm that so attracts him. "It would be my pleasure as well."

They meet most afternoons, Charles Willson painting unusually slowly, to keep hearing her low voice, to keep watching the ripples of emotion across her calm face. As he paints, he asks and learns that she teaches free Black children; helps her mother, as they have no servants; finds her greatest joy in music. What he hasn't learned is why she isn't married; young men, too, must have been attracted by her quiet grace. He reasons that beauty may have come to her as she's aged. In any case, he's charmed as they talk, writing of sittings like this in the autobiography he's begun:

The portrait painter cannot but be sensible of the attractions of a lovely sitter, because he wishes by his art to make his imitatin as pleasing as possible, consistent with the truth, therefore he will exert his powers by conversation as well as by his knowledge of drawing and colouring to produce original beauty, and, if he cannot fall in love with his copy, yet he is in danger from the original, whose native charms he endeavors to develop.

He wants to never finish this portrait and fears that once he puts on the last brushstroke; once Hannah looks at what he's made of her, she'll feel diminished, or worse—he's come to have this sense of her modesty—feel he's falsely flattered her. Heart in his throat, he puts down his brush and steps away from the easel: "I hope I've done you justice."

She is as delighted as he could hope she would be; without exclaiming or showing obvious enthusiasm, without taking unseemly pleasure in her own appearance, she says: "It's a very good likeness, I think, although I can't really see myself," and puts her hand on his arm.

"A speaking likeness, would you say?"

"Yes, yes. I wouldn't have thought of it that way, but yes. . ."

"It's what I try for in a portrait," he answers, comfortable now to speak of his art instead of her appearance or the dangerous ground of his emotion.

As he wipes his brush on a well-used rag, and Hannah adjusts her shawl, he invents a reason to see her again, beyond merely asking if he can call on her sometime: "Would you like to join me and my daughter Angelica on a trip to Baltimore?"

Before she can answer, he elaborates: "My son Rembrandt has found a promising building for his own museum, and I'd like to see it. I'm not sure that city can support another museum so like my own, and I need other opinions."

He flushes, fearing he's said too much, or not enough to convince her. But Hannah asks serenely: "When would you like to leave?"

His mind races so frantically he's sure she can see his desperation; he has to reserve places on the packet boat, find a place for them to stay. "Next week?"

"How long will we be gone?" With her *we*, he hears that she'll join them.

"Three or four days. The boat alone takes eight hours."

"I'll ask another teacher to take my pupils." He notices that she doesn't say she has to ask someone's permission; clearly, she's used to making her own decisions. "Let me know which days, and where I should meet you."

Inviting Angelica along was a happy accident of inspiration; she's thrilled to travel and flattered to be asked her opinion. Charles Willson has described Hannah as a friend with an interest in museums—a white lie that troubles his conscience, but not enough to make him abandon it. When they meet at the slip where the packet boat is tied, each woman is pleased by her first impression: Hannah by Angelica's generous, rosy beauty; Angelica by Hannah's calm warmth. Hannah leans forward to kiss the younger cheek; Charles Willson is startled that his plan is moving forward so fast.

The trip through the mouth of the Susquehanna is rough; Hannah stays in the cabin with the pilot while Charles Willson and his daughter delight in the wind and spray on deck. When they dock in the inner harbor and descend the gangway, it seems natural that Charles Willson will offer Hannah his arm, and that she will lean on it, ruefully mocking herself: "I'm glad to be finally here!"

Charles Willson has written to ask old friends of his and Rachel's, the Bordleys, if his party can stay a few nights with them. He has no sense that the arrangement, even the request, might be awkward for anyone, especially Hannah, but as far as her reaction goes, he's judged right. She responds to their welcome, while they're relieved to see their old friend with such a steady woman, after the volatile Eliza. No one has mentioned the future, but, on this visit, it's understood. Before they leave, Mrs. Bordley hugs Hannah impulsively: "I trust you with his children."

The sea is calmer on the trip home; Hannah agrees to sit on deck with Charles Willson, enjoying the breeze that lifts the hair that escapes her bonnet.

Charles Willson sits close to her, with half his attention on the water, determined to keep her secure there. He finds himself talking about his fears for Rembrandt's new effort—How well will Baltimore receive it? Where will he find his collections? (meaning: *Will he compete with me? Why is he doing this?*)—almost as freely as he talks to Gloriana, and more volubly. Hannah encourages him by her quiet attention, her questions that go to the heart of his concern:

"Are you afraid his museum will replace yours?"

Angelica, who has been only half-listening, sits up straight as Hannah continues:

"You're so well established as an artist and collector you shouldn't worry that anyone else will replace you."

And then, so mildly that it doesn't seem like a rebuke:

"Your son needs to be free of you."

Chapter 28

THE FIRST TIME HANNAH COMES TO DINNER at Belfield, she comes with her parents. Charles Willson has been in the kitchen so often, tasting sauces, testing the roast for doneness, asking Mag a dozen times if the lettuces are washed, that Peggy finally banishes him to the dining room, where he arranges and re-arranges the flowers Isba has picked. She shouts at him: "Father, please!" and instead of admonishing her, he slinks into another room, abashed.

The younger children are supposed to set the table, which they do by arguing, one boy rearranging the forks and knives Angelica has carefully placed next to the dinner plates.

"When will they ever come?" Franklin's question is so loud that those entering the hall have heard it.

"It seems we're late," Mordecai Moore, who is always aware of the exact time, announces, while Hannah's mother exclaims: "Oh, dear," and Hannah reassures both of them.

Although Angelica has warned the younger children to be quiet and behave when the guests are there, they've had little guidance in what *behave* might mean. Franklin and Linnaeus run into the hall to stare; Titian II is off, as usual, watching frogs at the pond.

Rag-tag is a phrase that might have been invented to describe this band of children—hair uncombed, clothes needing a wash, hems unraveling—but Hannah strikes exactly the right note, shaking the hand of each in turn, as her mother steps back, pulling her skirts aside as if the children might contaminate her.

The meal proceeds despite spilled water, jostled elbows, kicks under the table, and not enough trifle for dessert, after Linnaeus missed the signal Mag was sending and took a double helping. Charles Willson talks non-stop about the dam he plans to build, the mill, the grain he'll grow to be ground there. Mordecai, the banker, asks, "How much grain will you need to sell, and at what price, to pay for all the labor going into this?"

"Ah, that's the problem! None of my boys here at home are big enough to help with a project like this; the others are off exploring the world. My friend Jefferson has a solution, but it's not one I can endorse."

Mordecai nods approvingly: "You disapprove of slavery, sir?" He can't help casting a skeptical eye down the table at Moses.

"I manumitted Moses' parents as soon as I knew they could make good livings. The boy will be free when he's twenty-six."

"In how many years is that?"

"Eight, no nine," Charles Willson is flustered, not expecting such direct questions, and flushes when from his place along the table comes Moses' clear: "It's eight years, Charles Willson."

Mordecai means to sound reassuring when he offers: "Sir, if you have to go before the Friends, the questions will be harder than this," but Hannah is quick to cut him off, unusually flustered in her turn: "But no one has said anything about Charles Willson coming before the Meeting, Father."

Mordecai wipes his mouth with his napkin to hide his smile.

As the Moores take their leave, Titian, mud-streaked from exploring the pond, presses something damp and gritty into Hannah's hand. She doesn't recoil but examines the treasure: a deep gray stone with a band of white around its middle.

He looks up at her expectantly and she doesn't disappoint. "It's a lucky stone; it will bring good things to anyone who carries it." Hannah's nurse found such stones for her when she was a child. "Would you like to keep it?"

"No, Miss; it's for you," Titian says, while Charles Willson beams but also can't help intervening: "Go wash it off, Titian: quick, before they leave."

Charles Willson and Hannah have hardly spoken of a shared future but are so at ease with each other that it occurs to neither that a question needs to be asked and an answer given. When Charles Willson asks to visit her father, his intention is clear. Mordecai is willing to receive him, but cautions: "Our local Friends must approve your union. It's not up to me to *give my daughter away*. She's not mine to give. "And," he adds pointedly, "you should know that the marriage ceremony is mostly silent."

One of Charles Willson's best, most redeeming, if rarely exercised, qualities is his ability to laugh at himself: "That will be hard."

"The Friends will give you ample opportunity to answer their questions when you meet with them."

In the wide circle of sober faces, somber colors, Charles Willson has unknowingly chosen a seat that the morning light coming through the high window picks out. It's not enough that he's pinned by the questions—about his marriages, his farm, his finances, his children—but that the light has fixed him so unsparingly that his flaws—the long nose, slightly pinched mouth, thick middle—are set in high relief. Hannah sits across from him, on the other side of the shaft of light; he can't discern her expressions as he talks about his love for Rachel, his grief at her death, his struggles to maintain the farm, to pay fair wages. Is he meeting the Quaker ideals he's hastily read up on: integrity, equality, simplicity, community, stewardship of the earth, peace? He's dressed as plainly as possible; his museum fosters community; his farm helps the earth; he left the Continental Army after Valley Forge and opposes war. . .

This is the first question, which comes with an edge of challenge, not the usual admiration, "You fought with Washington at Valley Forge, sir?"

"Yes, and so did my brother James. After that, I laid down my gun." *James, bearded and bloody, wrapped in a blanket, unrecognizable, calling his name.*

He senses Hannah sitting up straighter, she's seen Rubens heading for the garden with a rifle on his shoulder. He rushes to explain—"We have a rifle in the house, left by my first wife's father. My boys use it to shoot groundhogs"—and stops short, feeling he's said too much, or not enough.

A woman he vaguely recognizes as a neighbor, although it's hard to see her face clearly past the shield of her bonnet, asks: "Why did you marry so soon after the death of your first wife? And why do you marry now, so soon after the death of the second?"

He can't confess the sexual ache to these stern judging faces, acute as his hunger for food, that afflicts him, that visits to Gloriana can't assuage. He wipes his sweating forehead with his handkerchief and searches for an acceptable answer; in the pause before he finds one, the woman persists: "You know that Friends tell the truth at all times?"

"My children," he says slowly, "need a mother. The house needs a woman."

Then a man he hasn't noticed leans forward: "Do you oppose slavery, sir?"

"I do, of course. I fought for abolition when the Legislature voted. My side lost; we had to compromise on manumission."

"And did you continue for work for abolition?" The words pin him to his seat; even though the light isn't falling on him, he feels exposed, and stammers: "I—tried to work in less contentious ways."

"But did you ever own slaves yourself?" the same man persists.

"I manumitted Scarborough and Lucy as soon as they could earn their livings."

"And their boy?"

"I will manumit Moses when he reaches twenty-six."

"And have you held any other persons?"

And Lydia is here, standing next to Rachel in the doorway as he left. *I don't know what I would do without her,* Rachel wrote. Would they have freed her after the baby was born? Would they have freed her if she hadn't died?

He will disappoint Hannah if he lies, disappoint her if he tells the truth. "Yes", he answers, his voice so low that the circle bends closer to hear him. "Yes, a young woman who helped my wife long ago. We would have freed her. . . . " His head lowers to his chest. *Everything is lost.*

The woman who has asked about his rush to marry asks now, "If Hannah is beyond childbearing age, what is the purpose of your union?"

He cannot see evidence of his loss in Hannah's face across the circle but imagines disgust in the slight motion of her head, as he makes his appeal: "I need her kindness to guide me in my home and my work. I sense in her the deep integrity that will complete me. . ." He feels himself floundering in syntax, foundering, when someone mercifully interrupts: "I think that will be sufficient, Charles Willson. We are all human. Hannah, what do you have to say?"

"I hope to be of help to my dear Charles Willson," she offers, and is met by a silence that seems, even to Charles Willson in his anxiety, to breathe assent.

The group meets later and approves the union, although some argue that Charles Willson hasn't opposed slavery sufficiently, isn't financially stable. "But their love is strong," the woman who had asked about the purpose of their union seals the decision.

When the mail coach arrives, with instructions for obtaining and signing a marriage certificate, Charles Willson, at lunch, throws down his napkin and rushes to detain and tip the coachman. Even before he knows what's in the envelope, he sees the thickness that signifies more communication than a simple refusal.

"Mrs. Honeywell, Mrs. Honeywell, it's good news," he babbles to his baffled house guest. Since she's the nearest person at hand, he grabs and hugs her: "Good news, Mrs. Honeywell, my friend. I'm to be married!"

For Mariah Honeywell, this is hardly good news; she'd had hopes of snaring Charles Willson for herself. She draws herself up, regal in her dismissal: "We will have to leave without further delay." She's been using the fever as an excuse to stay longer in his household, asking even the visiting Hannah what news she had of the epidemic, and packing and re-packing the things she'd brought.

Charles Willson, conscious of community good will though he is, doesn't try to dissuade her. Only Moses will be sorry to see the Honeywells go; he'll miss the intimate mornings with Martha: holding the bowl of *café au lait* gently to her lips, after testing its heat; breaking the breakfast roll into the right size for her mouth; watching and waiting until she's ready for the next bite, next sip.

"We've been a great team, Mo," she says on their last morning, and seeing the tears that brim and enlarge his eyes, reassures: "We'll meet again in the museum, my dear," and he runs from the room.

Chapter 29

THE WEDDING IS HELD in the same Meeting House where the interview took place, in the same circle of witnesses, who seem more friendly now that they've accepted Hannah and Charles Willson as a couple who have promised to love and respect each other.

"I hope," one woman offers, "that you and everyone you deal with will be honest and kind." Her hope seems a kind of blessing and is the last thought that can be said on the subject. After a long silence, there is first the rustle of a skirt, then the shoe-shuffle and chair-scrape of the crowd rising before it files out into the pale fall sunlight.

Charles Willson has invited the assembly back to the farm for lunch, but most have declined; it will be a modest gathering, although Lucy has been hired to bake a wedding cake. A ham has been cut down from the smokehouse, and all the vegetables still growing have been picked. Hannah, in her grave but warm way, compliments everyone: Lucy, Peggy, and Mag for their baking and cooking; the vegetable pickers for their choices; all the children for wearing their best clothes. She takes time to bend over Margaret Peale to make sure she's comfortable, and, in her presence, a calm settles over the company.

Even Charles Willson, at the head of the table, carves the ham more carefully, each slice as thin as paper, and talks less. The dishes are handed around more slowly; no child jostles another or snatches a bite from another's plate. It is as if peace has come to them all. Charles Willson raises his glass of cider, glowing in the afternoon light, but it's Rembrandt who offers the wedding toast: "To long life and happiness for my father and his wife!"

"And the same to my children, to everyone in this household, and our friends," Charles Willson answers, "with thanks for this meal."

There is a bit of music in the drawing room afterward—Angelica opens the harpsichord; Isba tunes her violin—but the few neighbors who've come hurry to leave the couple to their own devices, unsure what those might be but wanting to be tactful. Seated in their traps and carriages on their way home, the couples may wonder if Hannah can still have children, and if she and Charles Willson can still "enjoy each other," as one farm wife asks her husband, to be shushed with a laugh and the squeeze of a breast.

Charles Willson himself wonders the same thing: a thin wire of uncertainty runs through the room as the last notes of Handel thrum into silence. Angelica pinches out the candle on her instrument before the wax can flow onto the wood. It's Hannah, of course, who saves the moment from awkwardness: "We all must be exhausted. Thank you, dear Angelica and Isba, for your music, and now I must go to bed. Goodnight, dear children," she says, as if blessing them all, as she steps past the youngest ones, perched and listening on the stairs.

He'd never felt uncertain approaching a woman, unbuttoning his shirt as she slips out of her dress, but finds himself trembling before Hannah as she turns to face him in the candlelit bedroom.

She is so good, so pure, almost holy, maybe no man has ever touched her. What do I do? Will I scare her or hurt her?

"Dear," he begins, "you must be tired. I can sleep in the next room to give you your rest": too many words sticking like lumps of dough in his mouth, but she saves him, stepping to him and laying a hand on his chest. "Dear Charles Willson, I want to lie down with you," and so they move together to push aside the quilt.

Legs, arms, mouths: a smooth mingling, and when he enters her, no barrier—not the impediment he expected. She gasps and trembles, but not with fear or pain; she laughs with pleasure when he withdraws and lies against her.

"Did I hurt you?" he asks anxiously and stupidly, smoothing her hair back from her flushed cheek. He's never seen her hair, except the strands that slipped from her cap. It's thick and dark on her shoulders, threaded with silver that picks up the candle-light. He doesn't dare look at her breasts, for fear of embarrassing her, but feels them rise against his chest.

"No, no, but now I need to breathe," she laughs, then puts her hand on his forehead and changes her tone: "Please blow the candle out. I need to tell you a story."

In the long darkness, with no moon to mark the hours, she tells of a man who said he loved her and went to war—"The oldest story," she says ruefully. "I began to show I was with child, and was sent away until she was born. When she died a few months later, I came back to my parents' house. It was as if she'd never been. The day I learned my lover had died at Valley Forge, I learned he had a wife."

Charles Willson puts his arm around her shoulders in the silence, tightens it as he feels the sobs she can't suppress. They lie that way together for they don't know or care how long, until he feels her body relax and take the deep unconscious breaths of sleep. In the morning, her eyes are clear as she reaches for him.

———

She rolls up her sleeves and pitches into whatever needs to be done on the farm, asking Peggy, Mag, and Isba to direct her. She weeds and hoes, digs vegetables and preserves them, cooks and cleans: so busy that she hardly notices that Charles Willson has gone to the city, until with a look of joy, she sees him come home again. She becomes almost as good as Anna at soothing the younger boys, and settling arguments between the girls. No one has to be asked twice do her bidding.

"Do you mind my going so often?" Charles Willson asks one night in bed.

"I'm happy if you're happy," she answers.

"Is there too much work here?" he persists.

"It's work that needs to be done." She stops his mouth with hers.

Chapter 30

UNLESS IT'S LATE AT NIGHT into early morning, and he doesn't want to be seen, Raph always arrives in a clatter—of boots in the hall, luggage straps clanking, coat buttons striking the doorframes—as he greets Argus with a rough and unwelcome shake of the muzzle; and Mag, whose job it is to answer the door, with a hard kiss on the mouth. She pulls back, shaken, as he storms into the kitchen, calling "How's my Peg?"

"Drunk again, Raph?" She barely turns from her pie crust.

"No, just in love," he answers, pinching off a bit as she slaps his hand. "She's on her way on the next stage."

Peggy straightens up to face him: "Why weren't you here for the wedding?"

"I didn't know in time." He turns to the cabinet where she keeps the cooking wine. "I had a sitting—with the very beauty you'll meet soon enough."

Mag has come into the kitchen unnoticed; she shakes the greens the boys have brought and begins to wash them free of dirt under the pump. If she pumps hard enough, she won't hear any more words, but some filter through the rush of sound.

"We'll be having another wedding here, not of old people, but the young and beautiful. . . ."

"Does your father know?"

"He will soon." Raph raises his glass to the silent women at their work on his way out of the kitchen.

The tall young woman who steps from the stage is tired, dusty and bewildered. Raph rushes her into the house, around the grounds, showing off the gardens, the half-built dam, his father's painting room, as if he were responsible for all of them.

She barely has time to piss as carefully as she can in the outhouse, wash her hands and flushed face before she's hurried to dinner, and barely responds to Hannah's kind greeting and Charles Willson's friendly questions. "I'm called Patty, short for Margaret," she manages, and offers little more. Luckily for the conversation, Charles Willson knew her grandfather in the War, and has so many stories of that genial old man that Patty's silence is barely noticed.

Except by Mag, who after being abashed by the other woman's blonde hair and fair features, watches her closely with growing pity. When, after dinner, Raph grabs her roughly around the waist, Patty looks as if she'll drop from exhaustion; she doesn't even try to smile.

Hannah shows her to one of the spare rooms, not so far from Mag's that Mag can't hear the rhythmic thumping of a body on a mattress and the faint, protesting cries that only make the thumping come faster and harder.

Raph, who has fled his home and its responsibilities at every opportunity, oversees every part of his wedding celebration: from flowers to food to music to invitations. Cleaning and baking move into high gear against the two-week deadline. Peggy and Mag, Moses, Charlie, and Angelica, Isba, and the younger boys grumble but urge one another on. Rubens takes time off from the museum to direct them. Lucy is already engaged for another party but will stay up late making four tiers of wedding cake. Charles Willson hesitates when asked to conduct the wedding ceremony, but finds in Raph's request a chance to lecture this son on fidelity and kindness—which he brushes off literally, cuffing his father lightly on the shoulder, "Of course, of course, old man. What do you take me for?"

Any inclination Charles Willson has to anger dissolves under Hannah's sympathetic gaze: "Isn't it good Raph wants you? Good he's taking so much interest?"

"Control is what he's taking," Charles Willson grumbles, as the work goes on.

Only Rembrandt, about to sail for France, stays away.

Isba has filled the house with vases of chrysanthemums and decorated the doorways with garlands of asters. She's made a circlet of bright leaves which tremble on Patty's hair as she walks into the drawing room where Raph waits, smiling with confidence. His hair, for a change, is combed back and tied with a velvet ribbon at his nape. The glass of hard cider that usually fills his right hand waits on the harpsichord until Charles Willson's few words of blessing are done, and Angelica, Isba and Moses take up their instruments to sound the notes of a Purcell recessional, then a Mozart minuet. Raph takes his bride's hand, swings her around and holds her to him with a deep-in-the-mouth kiss, which startles her and delights the crowd of Raph's friends, who clap as the dance begins.

The formal lines quickly break down into exuberant free forms, driving the older dancers off the floor and into the dining room. After the feast and the carving of the cake with Charles Willson's 1776 sword that Raph has found in the back of a closet; after the toasts to Patty, her parents, and everyone in sight, and to Peggy and Mag in the kitchen, to Lucy at another party, to Moses, and to the absent Rembrandt, Raph leads Patty to the stairs, and slaps her buttocks as if she were a barmaid he's just met. "Up you go; I'll join you later."

She stumbles and holds tight to the railing; Mag catches a glint of droplets on her cheek as she climbs. Charles Willson and Hannah have loaned the bridal couple their bedroom, with its bay window and wide view of the sky. "If you need anything, dear," Hannah offers, "let me or Mag know," while Mag hides her dismay behind the pile of soiled napkins she's retrieved from the table. Patty doesn't answer, taking the stairs as upright and determined as if she were Anne Boleyn on the scaffold. Watching her ascent, more guests than Charles Willson shake their heads.

Raph takes over the playhouse, leading his band of friends, and ordering Moses to bring more drink. "Oh, and tell Mag to bring more candles."

Moses rolls a keg of cider across the grass and hesitates to ask anything more of Mag: hesitates with an unease he couldn't articulate if asked. "Thanks, boy," one of Raph's friends says, insulting in a way no one in this house countenances, and Raph, not noticing, repeats: "Tell Mag: those candles."

She staggers with the weight of it—the candelabra is silver, a treasure Rachel's mother buried during the War—holding it in her good left hand and supporting that with the stub of her right. The candles list in their holders as she moves over the rough lawn; the matches in her pocket bang against her thigh. Peggy has called as she was about to light them: "Wait till you get there; you don't want to set your hair on fire!"

"Oho, my girl!" Raph takes the candelabra from her, and pulls her into the playhouse, where his friends are gathered around the keg. "Let's see what you've brought us! Light this, one of you, and I'll light this. . . ." putting his hand on her breast and grabbing the neckline of her dress. One of Angelica's or Isba's cast-off muslins, washed to translucency, it tears to the waist at his touch. Mag's breasts, white and unprotected, goose-bumped, tremble in the light.

"Who wants first crack at this?" Raph turns to his circle of leering friends.

"She'll enjoy it, I can tell you."

Stunned, flushed red, Mag stands frozen to the spot, unable even to hold the torn edges of her dress over her chest.

"Don't touch her." Moses is in the doorway, seeming taller than she's ever seen him, his face made of stone. Raph starts to toy with him, "What're you doing, boy?" and then notices Rubens at Moses' back. Moses pulls off his jacket, puts it around Mag's shivering shoulders, and helps her to the house, holding her close to his side, matching her wavering steps to his.

Rubens stares for a long, charged moment at his brother, and turns, shutting the door, hard, in his face.

When Peggy sees Mag's face and torn dress, she doesn't need details. "Get blankets," she orders Moses, and, to Rubens, says, "You'll need to tell Charles Willson." She makes a cocoon of blankets next to the stove and settles Mag into it, smoothing back her hair but not trying to take off her torn dress. She'll sleep the night next to her.

Charles Willson and Hannah appear in their night clothes, rumpled and alarmed, both looking older, wrinkled by sleep. "Where is he?" Charles Willson asks without preamble, but before his father can dress and find him, Raph is there, drunk and contrite: "I was only joking."

But Rubens shakes his head, and Charles Willson ushers Raph firmly into the library and closes the door. What Charles says that night he's said and written before and will repeat in his letters to Raph in the years to come: about his responsibility to Patty, to his children, to himself:

"*Like myself you may not always possess entire command of the appetite.*"

Later, when he and Hannah finally lie down together, close in Angelica's borrowed bed, he expresses a pessimism he hides in front of almost everyone:

"I don't know what will become of him. Or of that poor girl he's married."

Hannah starts to utter the familiar platitude of her faith: *I wish everyone could be honest and kind*—but quickly realizes it doesn't apply here, and will only serve, in its irrelevance, to show her lack of understanding; she simply puts her hand on his chest, moving the nightshirt aside.

Charles Willson's sleep is deep and refreshing; Hannah's less so. She worries that she's being dishonest when she lies: "Yes, I had a lovely sleep," and shifting under him as sunlight fills the room. *"My time,"* he'll write in his *Autobiography, "would be very heavy without her."*

Mag, for her part, unwraps the blanket Peggy has put around her and insists on carrying on as usual with the morning's chores. When Moses brings fresh water from the spring, she says simply, "Thank you," and he nods, "Of course," which becomes an unspoken pledge. Over the next weeks and months, they hardly speak, but move in concert: Moses sensing when she needs an extra hand or two to carry a roast or lift a pile of wet sheets or stack of dishes. She never has to ask for help or decline an offer on the days he's not at the museum with Charles Willson.

One evening, he comes in elated: Charles Willson's niece, Sarah, has asked that he cut her profile because of the way he adds details of hair, collars, necklaces. She, and he, are especially pleased with hers: the waving strands of hair that escape her cap, the ribbon tied at her throat. Moses has given the profile a background he painted blue; like *cornflowers,* and instead of signing his name, prints MUSEUM at the bottom, to make it seem more official.

Sarah pays the usual fee, even though her uncle has waived it, and gives Moses something extra besides.

Other evenings, Moses is subdued; Mag senses that more customers have chosen Martha for their profiles. If he gave her an opening, Mag would ask whether they chose her out of curiosity more than a perception of skill. She wants to reassure him and can only enter their unspeaking choreography, as they work to bring dinner to the table, clean up, secure the house for the night. If they touch, it's by accident: the brush of elbows or shoulders as they lift and carry.

The evening he comes back with the traces of tears glistening on his cheeks, she breaks their pact of silence: "What happened?"

He sinks into a chair by the stove, although it's time to bring the dinner dishes in. "It's Martha. She's getting married."

"Who to?" Mag stops slicing the bread and holds the knife up in her surprise.

"A good-looking man. White," he says, his voice so low it's at the edge of her hearing.

Peggy comes into the kitchen to ask where the dinner is, catches the tone of the conversation, and picks up a dish herself.

"What is he like? What does he do?" Mag, with her new sympathy for Martha, worries that this man is simply a trifler, a curiosity-seeker, heart-breaker, but Moses struggles to be fair:

"People say he's kind. Good as he looks. Also rich."

"Sounds too good to be true," Peggy catches the gist of the exchange, and breaks in.

"I hope not," Mag surprises them both with her firmness, and Moses stares at her, as if by looking hard enough, he can understand her.

"I thought you hated her," he ventures, as if they still shared their childhood confidences.

As if that confidence had never faded, she answers, "No, I began to understand her."

It becomes their habit without either of them realizing it: After the kitchen table is cleared and the food left from dinner is put away, Mag brings her book and often her notebook and pen, to read or write until the candle sputters and she finds it hard to hold her head up against the pull of sleep. Moses joins her with paper and a stick of charcoal, drawing a bowl of fruit or a vase of flowers: whatever happens to be in front of him.

Sometimes he counts the money he's earned from profiles; sometimes he tells her about the customers who ask to have their bulbous noses made slim and straight, and the ones who cry when they're surprised by a beautiful result. One evening when Charles Willson finds them there, he teases: "Has Moses told you about all the girls who can't stay away from him?"

Mag is startled to feel stabbed in the heart; she's never thought anyone would take him away from her. He's become so much a part of her that she's never noticed how his black eyes glow in his brown face, how his cheekbones cut the air, how his long fingers handle with grace whatever they hold.

One evening when he doesn't come back from the city, Charles Willson jokes, "We'll have to keep an eye on that rascal," and Mag feels she's already lost him.

She takes her notebook to her bedroom, wanting not to be watched or interrupted before she can write:

I'd just noticed the violets in the grass
and then I saw them crushed
beneath some heavy boot sole

Just three lines she doubts anyone will read, but the weight on her heart lifts. Is she writing about Raph or Moses? Both or neither? Should she describe the violets' delicate petals and heart-shaped leaves, or is this enough, this shape in the air, *against* the air? Somehow, it's what she wanted; she hides her notebook under the linens in her drawer and slips under the quilt.

When Moses comes back the next evening, she concentrates on all that needs to be done for dinner, although he tries to catch her eye. She even refuses his help lifting the heavy capon out of the oven, and would have dropped it if Peggy hadn't been passing by. "Mag, you know to ask for help; we could have lost the dinner."

Close to tears, she douses the burn on her forearm with cold water, furious at herself and confused. If anyone wonders why she bends to her plate throughout the meal and offers only a mumbled *please* and *thank you*, no one is tactless enough to ask. When she brings her book to the kitchen table in the after-dinner stillness, Moses takes a seat at the opposite end. She reads; he draws in a silence neither is willing to break, until he slides his paper down the table to nudge her book.

"What's this?" She's the picture of disdain.

"It's you," he answers and gets up to leave without waiting for her reaction.

He's only had a stick of charcoal but he's captured her heart-shaped face and up-tilted eyes, the tumble of her dark hair: drawn her as loved.

"Moses," she calls to his back, but the door swings to behind him.

Chapter 31

WITHOUT QUITE REALIZING it and certainly without discussing it, their lives braid back together. They begin to talk about what they hope for, what futures they imagine, although without seeing those dreams as combined.

"I have five years to go before I can be free." Seven notches on the milk room wall.

"Why so long? Why not just ask Charles Willson?"

"I know what he'll say. I have to be twenty-six; Charles Willson goes by the book." The twist of his mouth makes clear that this isn't a compliment.

"Still, you can ask, can't you?"

"It'll look like I'm not grateful."

"But then you could work when you want to and wouldn't have to wear that on your head," pointing to the turban he's torn off after wearing it all day at the museum. "Unless you wanted to."

"It must look pretty silly. . ."

"No," she doesn't say the exotic costume makes his good looks even more striking—won't give him that—but allows: "I can see why all those silly girls like you."

The wig on his balding head,

the long stockings hiding his ropy veins,
paint that covers the pox marks

She writes in her notebook, taking it to the library in the hope of finding Charles Willson napping there. The lines aren't what she wants to write about Charles Willson, or even part of it, but she likes the cross scratch of her quill on the page.

When he wakes to find her there, the glasses on his opened book slip to the floor, where she leans to retrieve them.

"How are you, my dear?" he asks through his after-nap daze.

"Well enough, thank you."

"I haven't apologized for Raphaelle." He struggles to sit upright, feet searching for his slippers.

"It's Raph who should apologize." In this moment when she's more certain than he, she presses her advantage: "Sir, I've been wondering why you can't free Moses before he's twenty-six?"

"Why, has he been wanting to leave Belfield?"

"I think he'd like to be free."

Charles Willson starts to argue his case, with all the indignation of the well-placed when their good intentions are questioned: "But would he have the same opportunities? He's making good money. . ." And then, under her cool stare: "I'll see what I can do." Then: "Has he been complaining?"

"No, but I wonder if he feels silly in that outfit. And hot."

"Now that Martha Ann is leaving, we have to make people excited about visiting the museum."

"She's leaving?"

"She's having a baby. . ."

Neither of them asks their question aloud: *Will the baby have arms, and hands, and normal feet?* And Mag has the same questions about herself:

And I ever dared

have a child, will it
be like me, and should I
want that

She props her notebook on her windowsill and writes to the unjudging sky as soon as she's free to be alone.

As Hannah and Charles Willson make their life together, her earnest calm is leavened by the rush of his enthusiasms; his ebullience is tempered by her serene confidence. Even as Charles Willson wonders whether to sell the farm and hurries to ready the museum for a grand opening, the household's life settles to an even hum. The youngest children feel the change around them; they quarrel less and even help one another; the girls grow more confident of their looks and gifts; Rubens is proud to be designated his father's deputy at the museum.

Although it's been open to the public for months, Charles Willson decides that there must be an opening: with music, stilt walkers, a fire-eater he's heard of, jugglers, Moses in his costume, and fireworks, but not as many as those that exploded at his Celebration of the Nation in 1796. He's painting the Philadelphia skyline on muslin washed to translucency, to be carried through the streets: a "moving picture" with the museum building larger than all the rest.

He worries, "It'll never be ready; there's so much more to do."

Hannah soothes," You need to go ahead; it will be fine," and prevails.

The day is clear; the fiddlers tune their instruments, the barkers call out on street corners; the crowds fill the street in front of the building and surge in; Moses, guiding them through the doorway, loses count. Charles Willson stands in the Long Room, showing off the cases filled with specimens and the bones of the mastodon he's excavated from a farmer's field.

The visitors seem more interested in greeting one another than in the displays he's worked so hard to prepare, but at least they've shown up. Among the nodding bonnets and bowing top hats, he sees a pile of golden hair, or rather smells a familiar scent—of rosewater and something more exotic—and hears the rustle of silk skirts.

"Congratulations, Charles Willson," Gloriana says, holding out her gloved hand. He hasn't seen her in months, not since he married Hannah and felt so satisfied that he had no need to seek out her company. He should, he thinks guiltily, have told her of the change in his life, and kisses her hand instead of shaking it.

"I hope you're well," he begins awkwardly, and would go farther, except that she gives a small shake of her head—"You've done a marvelous job here,'—and quickly turns away, followed by a man that Charles Willson recognizes as one of the richest in the city: a banker and official: short, with dark brows and deep-set, deeply pouched eyes that look intently at the man before him.

"You've done the city a great favor, sir," he says, before disappearing into the crowd after Gloriana. Charles Willson babbles his thanks and wishes he could have added: "I hope the city will find a way to support us."

It will be his refrain over the years, as he appeals to the city, to the nation, receiving sympathy from his old friend Thomas Jefferson but no material help.

That summer Charles Willson writes again to Jefferson: *so dry a season. . .The springs generally failed, and many families in Germantown were obliged to send for Water to the Creek or the Run supplying our Mill. My Spring House water stagnated & the fish pond perfectly dry...*"

The drought and the work that must be done on the mill bend his mind toward selling, as more friends and acquaintances send specimens for the museum: *The rooms I now hold are crowded with interesting articles of every denomination:* some animals to be skinned, stuffed and mounted without delay. He has too much to do on every front, writing: *in my fancy for getting everything that I have conceived might be convenient or useful I have indulged that fancy to its fullest extent —and my fault has been more for attempting to make what I wanted than imploying my time in a more profitable profession which would have given me the means of paying liberally to a better mechanic than myself —and my only consolation now is, that I have by my labours always make myself happy...*

But he confides to his diary that he needs to *get back to his pensil.* Of Hannah, he writes *my time would be very heavy without her.*

They will have eight years truly together, when the yellow fever, raging again that summer, attacks them both. Charles Willson treats himself, as usual, with herbs and rhubarb, and slowly recovers. In a separate room, the doctor tries to cure Hannah with blistering, but she *became worse... I had hoped from the stillness that they had given her an anodine to keep her quiet while the blisters was drawing— No the stillness was death—she died without pain.*

It's his most grievous loss, even more than Rachel's or the first Titian's. It takes a month for his fever and cough to lessen, and then both Rembrandt and Rubens come to stay with him, afraid he'll try to follow her.

Chapter 32

H E HASN'T FORGOTTEN HIS PROMISE to Moses; in fact, he thought of it constantly through fever, despair, and waking dreams. He's no stranger to public speaking, was a member of the Assembly himself; he knows how cautious his former colleagues are. Instead of making the case for freeing Moses when he's legally an adult, not waiting until he's twenty-six, Charles Willson asks that he be freed a year early.

He writes out a passionate argument and practices making it, all the while wondering whether he should go further, and wondering why he's doing this in the first place. Isn't it more convenient for him to have Moses at his side, in his home, for a few years more?

In the end, even taking a year off the requirement is a struggle between those who believe literally in *Life, Liberty and the Pursuit of Happiness* and those who fear that the laws they've so recently adopted are being weakened. The discussion in the Assembly becomes vehement: charges of *recklessness* thrown at Charles Willson, and of *sheer bigotry* that Charles Willson flings back, while flinching from the hostile, often insulting looks that drove him from politics years before.

The vote is close; Charles Willson can go home with qualified good news, shaken and sweaty, and worried that by this petition, he's ruined his chances of getting tax support for the museum.

"Good news," he calls out; Moses and Mag shout and hug each other before shaking his hand and thanking him repeatedly, before realizing that he has more to say. Moses still has four years to wear this yoke, light as it may seem in this household. He sketches another mark on the milk room doorframe: a pair of wings five spaces above the one he made the New Year's Day just past.

The years seem endless, busy as they are, but the space between his freshest mark and the wings begins to close with every January 1st, when Dr. Franklin comes with his "Persevere, children," and a gold coin for each of them. The girls and boys whose heads he used to pat have grown too tall and proud of their independence for such a gesture, but there is still a younger batch to receive his blessing. Mag and Moses always sense that the old man offers his directive to them with a particular emphasis. By the time they begin to exchange glances over the heads of the youngest boys, and Mag has to struggle not to show her disdain, the marks Moses has made on the doorframe have almost reached the wings he'd sketched there.

Mag waits to find Charles Willson dozing during his afternoon nap, waits, unable to read or take up her notebook, until he stirs and glances across the room.

"My dear?"

"Sir, Moses's birthday will be next Wednesday."

"Well, we'll need to give a party. Maybe Lucy will make a cake."

"Sir, he'll be twenty-five."

At that, Charles Willson sits up, and retrieves his glasses from his stomach:

"Indeed. I'll need to draw up the papers, he'll need to file them with the court. . ."

"And we'll want to marry now."

He stands and claps his hands: "Yes, a celebration!"

When she finds Moses hoeing in the garden and hugs him in his muddy clothes, she breathes in his ear, "Now no one owns you," but he draws back. "Only you," he says. "You own my heart."

Instead of a wedding ring, Mag will wear a copper bracelet that Moses has found and twisted to fit her right wrist. It is a "Belfield Wedding": Charles Willson presiding, Peggy and Lucy laying out the finest foods of the season; Rubens—grudging but willing—overseeing the boys' choices of the freshest greens; Angelica and Isba bringing in armfuls of lilacs and making a wreath of white violets for Mag's hair.

Charles Willson outdoes himself in his ceremonial speech: "I pronounce young Moses a free man, the best profile cutter I know, and our Mag the luckiest and loveliest of young women. I celebrate them as they make this union. . . . " And he loses his place, but with a nudge from Angelica, returns to his charge—"I now pronounce you, with pleasure, man and wife"—to cheers and applause.

Thomas, whom they all keep calling *Scar*, gives the parting blessing, wishing for them *All this world can give, and life-long love for each other*, before tuning his banjo and playing the plangent tunes he remembers: high, heartbreaking in their sorrow and hope, holding the household as if in a broad palm, in the knowledge that everyone will disperse and change.

Encouraged to drink as much as he wants, Moses has drunk more than he's used to. He and Mag stagger together toward the playhouse, when Mag drops his hand and turns back, to Charles Willson watching from the kitchen door. She stretches to her full length and kisses his cheek. "Thank you," she whispers, and darts away, to where Moses waits to lift her in his arms.

When he tries to carry her over the threshold of the place where they'll live until they leave this household—he drops her and collapses beside her, both in a burst of laughter. Barely inside, in their private place for the first time, they undress each other in hilarious haste. Without clothes, they're suddenly struck silent, staring at the bodies they've sensed for years and now are bare before them, dedicated to each other for comfort and pleasure. Inexperienced though they are, they take time with their hands and mouths, touching with the awe given a miracle: a long, sweet first night of what will be the *life-long love* Thomas has wished for them.

At dusk, in the after-wedding stillness, Charles Willson, who never pauses, pauses. Light from the kitchen shines a broad green swath on the grass. The fountain in the garden is too silent, he thinks, and stumbles on the path toward it, overgrown now that Rubens is no longer in charge of edging it. The bowl is thick with algae, and water has stopped flowing from the spout: another task to attend to, but not till tomorrow.

He turns back to the house; lamps are being lit in the upstairs bedrooms. The sturdy three-story structure floats on the fields, its dormer windows the look-outs. It's sheltered him and those in need of shelter: an ark.

The farm should be sold, but how can he leave it, in all its beauty and unrealized dreams? Not yet, not quite yet. . . There's still time to take up his *pensil* again, and write the story of his life.

Chapter 33

BUT STILL THE MILL-WHEELS and windmills need to be built to keep the farm alive, even as he spends more time at the museum. He hasn't paid enough attention to Angelica when she receives the attentions of Alexander Robinson, a young businessman from Baltimore. She fails to see that her suitor has no respect for art and artists and the love of dreams that has nourished her; he fails to understand how strongly she's tied to her family. When she accepts his proposal, she thinks his fortune will help save the farm; Alexander thinks only how amiable and generous she is.

Charles Willson paints their portrait as a wedding gift: Angelica, pleasingly round and rosy, her hair unbound; Alexander at an awkward angle, straining to be gone. The tension between her husband's frank dislike and her love for Charles Willson will keep her from the visits home she longs for. Her teeth will cause her pain all her long life; her letters to her father will record his attempts at new porcelain replacements and silver settings.

Sophonisba—*Isba* until she marries—will have the bad luck of fragile health but the great good luck of a loving husband: a businessman like Alexander, but one who loves her family as she does.

After Margaret Peale has slipped away, even strong Peggy weakens; Franklin and Linnaeus start telling their father they can run the mill and make a go of the farm. Titian and his wife, Elizabeth, offer him rooms in their Philadelphia house. With regret and gratitude, and a determination not to be idle, he moves in with his lathe, his printing press, a small wood furnace, and the carpenter's bench where he makes false teeth for friends and neighbors, embarrassing those in his family who see his amateur dentistry as demeaning for an artist of his stature.

Increasingly deaf, hating to ask his grandchildren to repeat themselves, he writes to Angelica: *"I often feel uncomfortable that I cannot with perfect freedom ask my friends to take a meal with me. But Titian and Elizabeth are very attentive to all my wants when they know them. Still I am like a fish out of water and nothing but my constant employment would make me bear it."*

Raph has traveled south to the scenes of his early success, leaving Patty to take in boarders and beg Charles Willson for help. In New Orleans and Charleston, Raph charmed his way into drawing rooms and receptions, also women's beds, but found no takers for his portraits or still life paintings, or even for the novelty of *trompe l'oeil* jokes.

He comes back to Philadelphia without telling anyone; a baker sends word to Charles Willson that his old customer Raph is in his shop, drunk, half-conscious, and about to be arrested. Father and children gather to take the prodigal to Titian and Elizabeth's.

Not moving, barely able to speak, Raph whispers to his daughter Eliza, "Tell Charles Willson that I respect and love him. . .I have not meant to hurt anyone." Eliza raises her voice so that her grandfather can hear, but when they turn back to the sickbed, Raph is dead at 51.

Not long after, word runs through the city, reaching even Charles Willson's weak ears: *The madam of Cherry Street has died. . .* He thinks, *with the last set of porcelain teeth I made for her in her mouth.* Part of his love of life, his lust, goes with her; he is an old man mourning in the funeral procession that winds through the narrow streets in the rain: all those who worked for her, those she sheltered: Black and brown women she saved from short, brutalized lives, beggars and outlaws who became her porters, butlers and partners.

He hopes she understood why his visits stopped after he married Hannah, is consoled by the memory of how wise and forbearing she was. He nods to the door-keeper he'd seen the last time he came to her house; the man's face is streaked with tears and rain. He reaches for Charles Willson's hand, and the old man pulls him into an embrace; the person and the time they've lost hold them there as the crowd breaks around them.

A quick smile, a warm glance, a graceful neck still catch his eye; at 86, he makes his last courtship, much to the amused dismay of this family—*What can he offer, living in one room? What is he thinking? Does she have money?* —and the darker memories of Eliza pregnant so soon after Titian's birth: *Can't he help himself?*

His granddaughter Sybilla comes every week to wash his hair, helping him tilt his neck onto the metal chute he fashioned years ago when the children were small. He talks to her about the promise of this new love as Sybilla begins to soap and massage his bare scalp and its ring of white hair, envisioning a new house, a new life. Then, while she carefully mixes hot water from the kettle with cold, he begins to doze and is fully asleep as the warm water sluices down the chute. Sybilla gently pushes his head upright and begins to towel it dry; he shakes himself awake.

"Thank you, dear girl."

Hair shining, clothes brushed, he makes his last visit to his new love on a bright winter day, and is staggered by her blithe smile more than her careful words: "Sir, I am honored, I am flattered, but my father thinks the difference in our ages is too great."

Rebuffed in his offer to speak with her father, stumbling down the steps, he wanders off-course on his way to the stagecoach station, misses it as snow begins to fall, and walks the six miles home. He's caught cold, is feverish, will seem to rally, and, in his delirium, wonder, *Did I do more good than harm?* He takes his last breath the next morning: February 22, 1827: gone, almost in motion.

His few belongings are parceled out among his children: to Titian, his feather bed and bolster, sofa, carpet, and razor; to Rubens and Rembrandt, his museums; to others, the unsold paintings, paints, odds and ends; and all that can't be measured: curiosity, energy, imagination, a love of the possible.

Most of his famous friends have died, but the funeral procession streams through the streets for blocks on a bright blue February day. Angelica and Isba aren't well, and Linnaeus is abroad, but all the family members who can get there are there: Rubens, Rembrandt, Titian, and Franklin, their wives and children, bundled in their winter coats; Raph's widow, Patty, grieving the loss of the father-in-law who helped her when Raph would not; all the artisans and farmers; portrait subjects and museum-goers; Martha Ann Honeywell, pushed in a chair by her husband; laborers and bar-keeps; landlords and tenants; Thomas Williams, who once was Scar, the best horse-trainer in the county; Lucy, known for baking the lightest Sally Lunn in the city; Moses, fingers stained from the profile he was finishing; Mag, now Lucy's assistant, and their children, who never knew Charles Willson and have to be shushed for their high spirits. Yarrow is there, and Antigua. The gravestone's inscription will read: "*Beloved by All Who Knew Him.*"

There's no room in the narrow parish hall for all the mourners, but they crowd in to shake a family hand, taste the pastries Lucy and Mag have made, and raise a glass. Coming home to their small house, when everyone is fed and asleep, Mag takes out her paper and pen, writes something there to join the other pages she keeps in her desk drawer: something she'll cross out and revise once and again, and keep hidden. One day a granddaughter will find and put them in a drawer of her own, until a descendant who writes poems too will bring them to light.

Afterword

THREE STERN PORTRAITS hung in a row, high in the stairwell in my grandparents' front hall, looking down on everyone who came and went. Two were of men I barely noticed; the third showed the woman my mother was named for: her great-great grandmother, Angelica Peale Robinson. As I climbed the stairs to explore the rooms where my mother and her sisters and brother lived when they were young, I thought Angelica Peale disapproved of me and everyone she saw. In the way that children absorb knowledge by being surrounded by stories, I came to understand that this great-grandmother of my grandfather's was the daughter of the Revolutionary War veteran, painter of Washington, Jefferson, and Franklin, and museum founder Charles Willson Peale. He named his children after famous artists and scientists: sons who were Rembrandt, Raphaelle, Rubens, Titian, Linneaus and Franklin; daughters called Sophonisba after the Italian Renaissance painter Sophonisba Anguissola; Rosalba after the Venetian miniaturist Rosalba Carriera, and Angelica after his contemporary, the English court painter Angelica Kauffmann.

Charles Willson Peale taught his children, nieces, and nephews to draw and paint. Many of them followed in his footsteps: Rembrandt as a portrait painter and museum founder; Raphaelle as a painter of still lifes; Titian as an artist-naturalist; Rubens as the director of the Peale Museum in Philadelphia. Their cousin Sarah Miriam Peale was the first American woman to make a living painting portraits.

My grandparents had only two Peale paintings: this portrait of Angelica, and a small still life of oranges painted by Sarah Miriam. My grandmother, who wasn't a blood relation, was proud of the Peale connection, while her in-laws, the direct descendants, disapproved. Charles Willson Peale's father was a convicted forger forced to choose between emigration from England to the colonies and a death sentence. Charles Willson himself worked as an indentured apprentice before he became an itinerant painter; he had many children and little money; he was also a passionate liberal and abolitionist.

When my mother inherited Angelica's portrait and Sarah's painting of oranges, they hung in our dining room: one a gloomy presence, the other a point of delight. When my mother died, and my brother and I divided her belongings, we agreed that I would take the Peale paintings (which weren't signed and so of uncertain value). A friend of my mother's told me to hang both at eye level, which changed my relationship with Angelica.

Her brother Rembrandt had painted her late in her life, probably in the 1870s. Her eyes are clear, calm, contemplative—hazel, like my mother's: a mix of green and light brown. The sense of loss I see in her now comes from what I've learned about her life: she suffered from toothaches, which probably explains her pursed mouth; she married a businessman she thought would help her family, although he disdained art and artists. He and her beloved father disliked each other, which made visits almost impossible. From a vibrant household of artists, she found herself defeated by her own good intentions, in a world of stifling conventions.

There's something about her presence, though, that conveys endurance instead of disappointment.

The Peales' legacy seemed an uncomplicated one: of artistic talent and achievement; of a commitment to the ideals of the Declaration of Independence; a belief in the abolition of slavery, and in education for all: founders of free natural history museums and the first secondary school for free African Americans. It was a shock when my daughter, concerned about racial justice and reparations, began to research the slave-holding of our ancestors in Southern Maryland, and beyond.

The Wikipedia entry for Charles Willson Peale began: "Charles Willson Peale owned slaves."

I was stunned. How did this stark statement square with his Revolutionary ideals and support for abolition? Why was Moses Williams, who made silhouettes in Charles Willson's natural history museum, described as enslaved?

Trying to reconcile facts with belief, I recalled something my mother had said, after reading Charles Coleman Sellers' 1949 biography: that Charles Willson Peale had been given an enslaved family as payment for a portrait. Given my assumptions, I'd dismissed it, believing that if Charles Willson accepted a payment in human beings, he would have taken this family into his own household, as he had taken in many others in need, and would have freed them quickly, into the thriving free Black community that existed in late 18th-century Philadelphia.

From my daughter's further research into the work of scholars and art historians of color, Gwendolyn DuBois Shaw and Asma Neeman, we learned the names of the enslaved family: Scarborough and Lucy; Moses was their son. We found that Charles Willson taught Moses, along with his own children, how to cut silhouettes for customers at his museum of natural history in Philadelphia but didn't teach him to draw or paint. It's not known how long Charles Willson held Scarborough and Lucy, only that he freed them in 1786. Moses, then eleven, stayed in the Peale household, enslaved, until he was twenty-five, a year short of the legal age for manumission in Pennsylvania.

I began to read all I could find about the Peales: in CWP's own voluminous writings and in art and cultural histories. In addition to contemporary critics who blame him for being a slave-holder, and for not teaching Moses to paint, feminist critics fault him for not staying at home with his first wife when she was about to give birth; David C. Ward portrays him as mechanically driven; and poet Susan Stewart finds him to have been afflicted by "fugue states" and compelled to collect objects for his museum to fill an emotional void. Other critics suggest that he was responsible for his son Raphaelle's early death. Emma Rutherford, in her introduction to *Silhouette: The Art of the Shadow*, sees his contradictions in the context of his time, while Carol Eaton Soltis, in her comprehensive *The Art of the Peales*, shows an astute attention to history and psychology, as well as to the fine points of painting.

I've tried to imagine what Charles Willson Peale was thinking, how he made his decisions, and what his household might have been like in the late 18th and early 19th centuries. I knew that he saw Belfield, the farm he bought as an "Arts Retreat" outside Philadelphia, as a refuge. That he believed in equality for all, and yet was a patriarch and a slave-holder, are contradictions that have troubled this country from its beginnings. This farm, based on idealism, would have been an island, surrounded on all sides by the brutal realities of slavery.

I wanted not to defend an ancestor, but to explore his family's life. Almost all of the characters existed, although very little is known about some of them. Charles Willson wrote constantly— letters, journals, and an autobiography—and left paintings of Washington and Jefferson that are valued today. Rembrandt, Raphaelle, Rubens, and Titian Peale are known variously for their work as painters, museum directors, and documentary naturalists.

Charlie, Charles Peale Polk, also became a painter, although not as famous as his cousins.

Moses became known for his vibrant silhouettes; of his later life, the record shows that he was able to buy his own house in Philadelphia with proceeds from his profile-cutting, and married the Peales' "white cook named Maria," with whom he had at least one child, a daughter. Some historians say that he lost his livelihood as photography became popular, lost his house, and suffered from alcoholism, or perhaps from neurological damage from the preservatives he used as a taxidermist in Charles Willson's museum of natural history.

The "white cook" of Peale history I've imagined as Mag. Scarborough and Lucy, who barely appear in history, have become important characters. Peggy Durgan and Margaret Peale, only figures in a family portrait, have more agency here. Martha Ann Honeywell was an artist with extraordinary physical disabilities and artistic gifts; she cut profiles in Charles Willson's museum. She also made remarkable collages, one of which is in the American Collection at the Metropolitan Museum of Art.

Yarrow Mahmout was a distinguished free Black property-owner and stock-holder whom Charles Willson painted; the only portrait he made of a Black person known to exist, and also one of the most expressive. Gloriana, the members of the Slave Patrol, the Randolphs, Antigua, and Anna are all invented.

The novel's setting is the farm Charles Willson bought later in his life, but the essence of events, the personalities, and family dynamics are based on the facts as I know them.

Shrewsbury, Vermont
February, 2022

Acknowledgements

I'M GRATEFUL to more people than I can count, but here are some of them:

My ancestor, Charles Willson Peale, for being such an interesting person;

My daughter, Anne, for her curiosity and her conscience;

My late friend Yvonne Daley, whose first response to hearing about this book was a simple, "Wow!"

Readers of an early draft, my cousins Lucy Howard and Steve Howard, for their keen sense of history and their discernment;

My Warren Wilson MFA writer friends: Andrea Barrett, David Haynes, Glenis Redmond, and John Skoyles; and fellow Vermonter and Four Way Books author, Sydney Lea, for agreeing to read and comment on *Belfield*;

Shrewsbury Library's Famous Books Book Club, for instructive discussions of classic fiction;

Writer, artist, friend and brilliant editor, Penelope Weiss, for her astute suggestions and support;

Longtime friend Grace Brigham for sharing her artist's gifts with such generosity;

The Shrewsbury Agricultural Education & Arts Foundation, especially Project Director Stephen Abatiell, for his interest and skill;

Vermont friends Phyllis and Michael Wells; and Terry, Vickie, Seamus, and Avery Martin, for always having my back;

The Castillo family, for all their help;

And Green Writers Press publisher, Dede Cummings, for her steady enthusiasm and beautiful book design. It's been a long road, but I'm glad we're coming to the end together!

NOTES

The Phillis Wheatley stanza on page 103 beginning, "Should you, my lord, while you peruse my song," that Mag recites to Scar come from the poem, "To the Right Honourable WILLIAM, Earl of DARTMOUTH, His Majesty's Principal Secretary of State for North America, etc." as reprinted in Phillis Wheatley: *Complete Writings, Edited and with an Introduction by Vincent Carretta*. New York & London: Penguin Books, 2001, p. 40.

Other lines of Wheatley's that Mag recites come from the same volume.

The fragment of a poem that she can't quite recall is, of course, Keats' sonnet, "When I have fears that I may cease to be."

About the Author

AUTHOR PHOTO BY STEPHEN ABATIELL

JOAN ALESHIRE was born in Baltimore, Maryland with limb differences. She grew up in a large extended family, hearing stories about their Peale ancestors. She began to read and write stories, plays, and poems. Joan graduated from independent schools, and from Harvard/Radcliffe in 1960. She studied film and Russian, married, worked on a therapeutic farm in Vermont, and had a daughter. The family moved to Brooklyn in 1966 and was active in anti-war politics. In 1973, Joan moved back to Vermont with her daughter, started a community library, and wrote poems. She received an MFA from Goddard College in 1980, became Interim Director of the Warren Wilson MFA Program, and was on the poetry faculty from 1983 to 2013. She has published six books of poetry; Belfield is her first published novel. In 2012, she started a non-profit to support small-scale agriculture in Vermont. She co-founded the Urban Farm Fund at the Baltimore Community Fund with family members.